Consequences of Attraction

Consequences of Attraction

Stories by
John Stewart Wynne

Consequences of Attraction: Stories by John Stewart Wynne

Copyright © 2025 by John Stewart Wynne

Published in 2025 by Tree Line Books (New York, NY)

Library of Congress Control Number: 2025920409

ISBN (Tree Line Books trade paperback): 978-0-931476-14-3

ISBN (Tree Line Books ebook): 978-0-931476-13-6

To learn more about the author, please visit *www.johnstewartwynne.com*

Visit the publisher at *www.treelinebooks.net*

10 9 8 7 6 5 4 3 2 1

*Dedicated to James Cunningham, Anthony DeFazio, and
in memory of John Oleksak*

Contents

A KILLING IN EAST HAMPTON

"DID YOU HEAR THAT somebody's been going around breaking into people's houses and smashing their computers and personal electronics to hell—not stealing them but destroying them ..."

That came as more of an incredulous statement than a question, posed to me by my husband as I weeded crabgrass from a row of carefully cultivated bush snap beans. They were growing tidily in the vegetable garden I'd started two months ago on the north edge of our ample back lawn in East Hampton. But there were some stubborn weeds among them.

"I'm not going to resort to using chemicals," I insisted as I dropped some into a potato sack, "not when I can yank them up by hand."

"Did you hear what I just said?"

I glanced up at my husband Scott standing right above me in the bright midsummer sunshine. His face was blocked by the glare. When I shaded my eyes, I not only saw his handsome face but his shadow elongated behind him, an imposing male imprint, rippling in the blades of grass stirred by the afternoon breeze just coming up off the ocean. I could be forgiven for finding his shadow sexy since I found everything about him sexy. We'd only been married six months and I couldn't get my fill of him. Two young men in love being able to get married was still pretty heady stuff.

"Why would anybody do that?" I asked. "It seems there isn't a motive of revenge. No one family's been targeted. They've all been random acts, haven't they?"

"It looks that way."

"Well, from what I've gathered they are." I'd read about the series of break-ins that morning in our East Hampton community-based weekly, *Dan's Papers*. "Purposeless acts of vandalism."

"And just plain stupid. There was nothing to gain financially." Leave it to Scott to be thinking about monetary motives in all things good and bad. He warned, "So when I'm at the office and you're here at the house alone, keep an eye out."

"I will." It was then I thought of our neighbor. I don't know why, it was just a gut feeling and I didn't have any proof. But ... no, I was being unfair. Warren was an older gentleman, a crotchety, independent thinker, an eccentric dismayed by the modern ways of the world, but he wasn't the kind to go around breaking into homes around East Hampton like some fleet-footed juvenile delinquent. Warren was in his late sixties and on the heavy side, had arthritis in both knees, and, an ex-smoker, he was always out of breath, but still managed.

I'd first met him two weeks ago during my long morning walk through our beautiful new neighborhood. I'd given up jogging, it was too hard on the body; I was definitely a convert to low-intensity exercises. I'd noticed his hunched figure on the side of the road, one hand up against a dying cherry tree, gulping air, his limbs shaking. That scared me. I didn't plan to blow out both my knees like the white-haired man gasping for breath in front of me. I walked up to him and asked if there was anything I could do for him. He put one hand up, either to stop me from asking additional questions or to let me know he was all right. Still trying to catch his breath, he pointed between a hedgerow at an elegant Georgian house set some distance back with a white rose-dominated garden in front of it.

"Oh, that's your house," I said. "I live one street over."

He smiled weakly.

I asked, "Can I help you inside?"

He finally answered, "No, thank you. I can make it." He pushed himself away from the tree, his face as dark red as the cherries that had dropped off and were sinking now into the wet and plump furrows of the earth. He found his own way to the circular drive and for a moment disappeared from my view. I waited a couple of beats before I peered between the hedgerows and watched as he haltingly made his way past the roses and up to the front door.

"I met our neighbor today," I told Scott that night at dinner. "An old white-haired man, heavy set. He has a beautiful home I must say. Over on Hither Lane."

"That's not his home," Scott advised me. "He's just the caretaker for the family who's spending the summer in Europe." Scott spoke with the calm assurance of the man who knew everything. He always made it his business to know everything.

"I see." So that was my neighbor. If I'd known then what I now know about him, I'd never have let our lives intertwine the way they did, I'd never have stopped and asked him if I could be of assistance. I'd have continued down the street enjoying my low-intensity walk, blinders on, and been much the better for it.

I unexpectedly ran into him a few days later, in the late morning, at a small grocery on Main Street where I'd stopped to buy a quart of orange juice. The place also served as a quasi-café that prided itself on its homemade sugary doughnuts, and—surprise—there was my friend sitting at a small table by the counter reading the new edition of *Dan's Papers*, an empty cup of coffee in front of him and traces of sugar on his face. He smiled and waved at me this time, a twinkle in his eye.

"Enjoying yourself?" I asked as I paid for the juice.

"Clearly," he said, wiping the vestiges of sugar off his face with a crumpled napkin. "Can I offer to buy you a doughnut, they have awfully good jelly ones, still warm."

"Oh, no, thanks. I have to watch my weight. I'm a newly married man."

"And so young!"

"I'm over twenty-one," I said. "But not by much."

"No, of course not," he replied. "Did you and your wife buy a house in the neighborhood?"

"We did. Four months ago. Only it's not my wife, it's my husband."

The old guy didn't miss a beat but motioned me over to him with the crook of his finger.

I sat down across from him. He was anxious to whisper to me that he was "gay" too, and then in a normal voice advised me he'd sensed I was "in the club" the first moment he saw me, but that it would have been "impolitic" of him to mention it at the time. I thought how he couldn't have mentioned it if he'd wanted to, he'd been so winded. He asked my name and I told him Ned and he seemed relieved.

"That's a good old-fashioned name, my boy. That was my best friend's name."

He told me his name was Warren and that he'd lived in this town, well, here or hereabouts, for most of his life, letting the busy world outside his "bailiwick" just keep getting busier. He seemed interested in what was going on closer to home though. "What house did you buy?" he asked.

I told him we'd bought the rust red cottage, that's what I called it, a street over from him on Middle Lane. It was a bit more than a cottage, of course, but that sounded cozy.

"I know it, the old Henley home. You're millionaires then."

I was surprised by his statement but why deny it or beat around the bush? You didn't purchase a home on Middle Street in East Hampton unless you had money. "Yes, we're millionaires."

One hand involuntarily went to his chin where he seemed to aggressively be trying to wipe more sugar off his face, only there wasn't any left. Realizing that fact, he dropped his hand in his lap as his face turned red like the other day by the cherry tree. He asked if he might know what my husband did for a living.

"He's a stockbroker."

That said, it seemed obvious, didn't it, that I had nothing more to do than tinker about Main Street during the day. He'd pegged Scott as the breadwinner which he was. But that was enough spewing out of my personal information. It was time to make a quick, low-key exit.

But Warren suddenly grimaced and clutched at his knee. It seemed likely he was faking this attack, probably because he wanted to keep me there talking with him. The guy was lonely, a caretaker in a house all by himself, wasn't he? Polite by nature and wanting to prove myself a good neighbor, I went the extra mile and asked nonchalantly if he'd walked from his house all the way up to Main Street. He nodded in the affirmative. I'd guessed as much. Could I offer him a lift home then? We lived a stone's throw from each other.

"Really?" he asked. "That would be extremely kind."

I drove along the sun-dappled lanes of East Hampton, just talking about the weather, nothing much else; he commented here and there, adding at one point how he couldn't even consider buying an automobile, the upkeep alone would do him in, and it seemed that in no time we were turning onto his circular drive. The roses, in full bloom, were shining like stars over the sun-splashed universe of sprawling green lawn.

"Come in a minute," he urged as I pulled up to the entrance.

"Well ..." I was curious about the house, I suppose. As I wavered, he clutched at his knee again and let out a yelp. "I'm all right," he assured me after taking a deep breath, holding it a moment before expelling it. Maybe he hadn't been faking in the grocery store and maybe he wasn't faking now; after all, the first time I'd seen him he'd been wincing in pain, one hand on that cherry tree for support. He had his copy of *Dan's Papers* on his lap. Our eyes went to the headlines which blared: BREAK-IN AT HOME ON EGYPT LANE.

Another one.

"May I read the article?" I asked.

"Of course." He handed me the paper.

The story stressed that although the recent string of break-ins had been contained in the Springs, a middle-class offshoot of East Hampton, this was the first time one had occurred in a more upscale area, a cause for alarm. "The house on Egypt Lane, it's just one street over," I murmured. "That's where the latest break-in occurred." Warren said nothing. I finished the article. On a night the family had been away from home, the vandal(s) had disabled the burglar alarm and gained entry into the study through a window on the ground floor. Three smartphones had been stomped on, an iPad had been "gutted like some hapless deer," according to the reporter whom I doubted had ever seen a gutted deer, an eighty-five-inch TV had been splattered with fecal matter, and an Apple computer had been found cleaved in two by the blade of a hatchet which had been left imbedded in it. A hatchet the family had never seen before. That was it. Nothing had been stolen. "Bizarre happenings," I summed it up. Warren said nothing. Again. In fact he acted like he hadn't heard me. Had he already read the story? Was he unconcerned about the latest incident?

"Well," I offered, folding the paper and handing it to him, "I'm sure the cops will catch the guilty party."

"Ned, you are coming in?" he asked.

I grinned. "Sure."

The house was immaculately kept, big airy rooms full of elegant, traditional Colonial-style furniture and high-quality antiques. The wood dining-room table and some of the chairs were Hepplewhites. I was no expert but I knew that much. I liked the rich details, the wreaths, shields, and scrolls above the elaborate fireplace and the soft beige and pink colors of the walls. Our house in comparison was contemporary, mixed and matched with Southwestern, Asian and Danish pieces and decor. Scott and I called our particular style "fusion on steroids." It was us. But could I get a sense of who Warren was from the decor? Not at all, the home wasn't his. And I couldn't get much from his affect either. He had his guard up, I sensed to protect some secret inside.

Warren guided me to his quarters, a three-room affair, a sitting room, as he called it, and a bedroom and kitchen. The sitting room had big glass doors that overlooked the back yard and the swimming pool. Two shirtless teenaged boys were cleaning the filters in the pool.

"What a burden," Warren lamented. "What drudgery to go through to attain the sparkling, crystal clear water Mrs. Labotte likes. Those boys, I'm in charge of them. They're friendly enough, but pretty useless most of the time. Mrs. Labotte would be better off to buy a self-cleaning salt/chlorine generator system and then fire the pool boys. But no, that wouldn't be charitable, would it? It wouldn't be right. They have to make a living too, like the rest of us." He eyed me pointedly and I nodded in agreement, a little embarrassed because I wasn't in the position to "have to make a living too, like the rest of us." A little embarrassed—but not much.

He banged on the glass and the boys looked our way; one gave Warren a thumbs up and the other a V for Victory sign. Warren held one hand up in mid-air as a response, the same gesture he'd given me yesterday when I'd asked him if I could help him up to the house, one that served both as an acknowledgment but also as a warning not to come too close. "I suppose they'll mow the lawn afterwards," he said. "It could use a trim."

The boys were hotties for sure, one golden-haired, the other dark, both with great builds and handsome faces. Creamy was the word that popped into my head ... sweet cream bubbling up, heated by the sun. If I wasn't here, I could imagine Warren closing the drapes, except for an inch or so, and peering salaciously at the boys while he got himself off. Or was he above all that? I noticed he had a stack of ten or so books on his desk, pages marked.

"I'm an avid reader," he explained. "I'm one of the most well-known patrons of the town library. I love it there. I spend all my free time reading."

There could be worse ways to spend time, I assured him. I'd almost said to kill time but had caught myself before blurting it out. To him reading was a proud vocation. I had a feeling it was his main passion in life, maybe his only passion. Had it always been? Had there been others? He brought me in a glass of iced tea and set a plate of pastries on the table between us and then he told me about the Labotte family who had employed him for the last twelve years. Apparently the husband was an ear surgeon who had come from a family of old money. They'd had three kids, but all of them were living elsewhere now, immersed in their own lives. They visited from time to time and brought the grandchildren. Mrs. Labotte in particular, Warren informed me, was his greatest champion. She had left for Europe fully confident he'd successfully oversee the affairs of running the property, and he began to list all his duties. I was bored stiff and found myself eyeing the boys by the pool, young studs plowing through the sunshine, battling the bright blue sky for prominence. While Warren's voice droned on and on. Just when I decided it was time to leave, his tone suddenly brightened and he asked, "My goodness, what does it mean for a young man like you to be married to another man?" He smiled at me and shook his head. "I can't fathom it, you see. Not at all. I must say I spent my life hiding in the shadows, the love that dare not speak its name kind of thing, concealing my Ned, the love of my life, from my own family as I watched my three sisters and one brother be married in the light of day."

Wow. I hadn't considered how different, I mean how incredibly different, his life had been from what mine was going to be. I sucked in my breath because it was breathtaking to consider.

"Observing them in their happiness," he continued, "but never being allowed to show them mine. Watching them open wedding gifts, reading notes of good cheer and well wishes from everybody, including me." His eyes sought the gold band around my finger. "Tell me, what is your ... your husband's name?"

"Scott. Scott Farrough."

I may have imagined it, it could have been a trick of the light, but I thought I saw tears well up in his eyes. Tears or not, he looked bereft.

"Look," I said, standing up, "why don't you come over and meet him? We're having a couple of friends over for dinner tomorrow night. Why don't you join us?"

He seemed shocked, as if he'd been invited to Buckingham Palace or the White House or something. "Could I? Do you think—" He shook his head. "No, I'd just be in the way."

"I'll pick you up tomorrow at seven."

THE NEXT DAY WAS Saturday. Scott and I met Kevin and his nine-year-old daughter Samantha at Two Mile Hollow Beach, the gay beach, and we pretty much stayed all day. It was only a few blocks from our house, in fact from our upstairs bedroom we were lucky enough to be able to hear the surf even though we couldn't see it.

Kevin and Scott had grown up in Sag Harbor together, best buddies, and they still were. Kevin was a successful realtor there and also a single dad who'd adopted Sam when she was almost one year old. Now she was an outgoing, bright girl at the head of her fifth grade class. Kevin had done all right with her.

Scott had lunch with Kevin a couple times a week since Scott's office was in Sag Harbor, even though he worked for an international broker whose headquarters were in the city. I don't know how Scott had talked his way into that one, getting to stay on the island and work, in the town where he grew up no less, but he was good at getting his own way, in business and in pleasure. As I stretched languidly on the towel I thought how I could hardly wait until tonight, after dinner, when everybody had gone home, to make love with Scott.

He talked Kevin into taking a walk down the beach. He realized it was no good asking me as I knew where they were headed and I wasn't interested. When Scott stood up, the guys lying within shouting distance stopped whatever they were doing and took notice. Well, they could eat their hearts out, I was the one married to Scott. He was stunning, tall and blond, with a golden body that was proud, conquering, full of fire: And God Created Man. Yes, later tonight ...

As I watched their figures getting smaller and smaller, before finally disappearing, I thought about going for a swim but the lifeguard's red flag had been up all day, meaning danger. Sharks, heavy undercurrents, jellyfish, riptides, something. Forget it, though the water looked so inviting. Sam was busy texting her friends and appeared to have no interest in me, so I took the opportunity to zone out to the sounds of muffled voices carried to me on the breeze and regularly interrupted by the breaking waves so I could never hear a full sentence, never put any narratives together.

I couldn't have been asleep for long. Scott's voice woke me. "You're sunburned," he said, then admitted what I already knew, that he and Kevin had walked along the beach in front of the exclusive Maidstone Country Club. Neither Scott nor Kevin's family were members and it was both of their goals to be asked to join one day. Not goals, burning desires.

"So you were torturing yourself again," I said to Scott, fumbling through my bag until I found the bottle of suntan lotion.

"Here, I'll do it," Scott said, grabbing it. He knelt behind me and massaged the lotion into my shoulders. It was so cold on my hot skin. "You've left it a little late."

"Thanks," I said. "I'm careless, aren't I?"

"More often than not."

"What's for dinner?" Sam asked.

"Swordfish," Scott said.

She made a face.

"Peanut butter and jelly sandwiches then," Scott revised the menu. "Whatever you want. Your wish is my command."

"You like fish," Kevin reminded her. "Living on the Atlantic coast you have to. It's one of our house rules."

"All right," she said, continuing to text away, "but not all fish. Remember when you ordered that horrible looking monkfish with the whiskers and stuff. Oh, God, Dad!"

"It wasn't that terrible was it?" Kevin asked.

"Wait! I'll bring up a picture of one and we'll see."

"No, that's OK," Kevin said. "We've got to get a move on. Pack up your things."

I, for one, didn't want to leave, sunburned or not. The golden glow of the afternoon was gone. The ocean was turning that strange shade of blue, a kind of wild dark sapphire, if a sapphire can be dark, and the sun was almost white.

"And you too," Scott told me. "Time to pull up stakes. You've had enough sun for one day."

"Yes, sir. Oh," I grabbed onto Scott's hand and he pulled me up. "I forgot. I invited Warren for dinner. You know, the caretaker at the Labottes."

"Oh? Him? What for?"

The exodus from Two Mile Hollow Beach had begun. The guys headed for the parking lot in a quiet procession, almost single file, lawn chairs and towels in hand, their day done. It was already chilly. Time to welcome the night.

"It's hard to explain," I said. "I think it was because I felt sorry for him being all alone. I'm not even sure now."

Scott kissed me on the forehead like an indulgent parent telegraphing that it wasn't important. But what had Warren said or done that had made me offer to come pick him up and drive him over to our house for dinner? The answer was lost forever in time. He'd simply be our guest at table tonight, sharing the evening meal.

It was a little awkward at first, Warren being there, sitting at the table, because I was the only one who knew him, but he was no bother, he was very quiet, almost afraid to speak. So we relaxed around him. Maybe we shouldn't have. It's a mistake to think just because your guest is quiet and well-mannered and doesn't say much that he agrees with what everybody else is saying or doing. That he approves of what's going on. I assumed he did. We're taught fairly early in life never to assume anything but I'd forgotten that rudimentary warning.

Kevin had made a big pitcher of strong Bloody Marys that we nursed through dinner, the adults at the table that is, Scott, Warren, Kevin and me, while Sam had her own pitcher of pink lemonade. Somehow with the drinks, dinner lost its importance and appeal but we toyed with our fish, sugar peas, and later, fresh raspberries. Scott and Kevin gossiped about someone Kevin had met on an online dating site, Kevin admitting that they'd texted each other ten times a day for the last week. The young man in question was a pharmacist already. Kevin brought up his photo and passed his phone around. He was in his mid-twenties and we all agreed he was a hunk, even Sam. All of us except for Warren who said nothing and passed the phone along without glancing at the young pharmacist.

"Maybe he'd be a good catch, Dad," Samantha suggested.

"You think so?" he asked.

Scott, busy bringing up stock quotes on his phone, said to Kevin, "Maybe it's time you found a man and settled down and got married. Then the four of us could go as couples on some pretty swanky vacations."

"Oh, no," Sam said, "you're not leaving me behind."

"That spoils everything," her dad teased, "having you tag along, spying on us."

There came that first subtle frown from Warren.

Sam jumped out of her chair and got into what I call a tech "jam session" with Scott, insisting on proving why her sleek new Galaxy Fold was way cooler than his iPhone. She flipped it open. "Bet your iPhone can't do this," she said, launching a 3D AR dance video from her favorite boy band, the stereo sound booming from the dual speakers.

Scott rolled his eyes. "Cool gimmick. They're still overpriced and constantly in the shop. The iPhones work just fine."

"You just like boring. Here ..." She showed us some shots she'd taken on the beach that afternoon including a breathtaking 3D shot of my husband, shirtless.

Again, Warren declined a look and there came the second frown, not so subtle now.

"Well," Kevin said to her, "I have something for your birthday next week."

"What, the brand new iPad Air with the M2 chip?"

"Yup," her dad said. "Light as a whisper, blazing fast, and in your favorite color, Blue Horizon."

"You get a whole bunch of free tryouts of the best streaming services with that, don't you?" Scott asked her, not looking up from his stock quotes.

But he did look up when Warren asked him, "Scoot?"

"It's Scott," my husband countered and took a calculated sip of his Bloody Mary.

"You don't mind if I go on my way, do you?" Warren asked. "I must say all of this technical talk is way over my head. It has me spinning."

"I'll teach you some stuff," Sam offered. "I'm a geek you could say."

"No, thank you," Warren said firmly.

"Well, I'll drive you home straightaway," I said.

Scott reabsorbed himself in his stock quotes and Sam sat down quietly on her dad's lap.

"Yes, well ..." Warren stood up from the dinner table. "Enjoyed it." He followed me outside and I drove him home. He gulped for air outside the car window. I noticed a full moon hanging over the trees, bloated and halfway sinister-looking.

"That's a blue moon," Warren said, heaving. "You know, 'once in a blue moon' ... They call it that, a blue moon, not because it's blue, but because it's the second one in the same month, a rare occurrence. Oh dear, I don't think your friend likes me very much."

"Who? Scott?"

Warren nodded.

"Why do you say that?"

"I didn't seem to know all about those gadgets everybody was using. I'm sure he thought I was backwards, old-fashioned."

I was sure he did too, but I lied, "He didn't even notice and he wouldn't care anyway. What difference does it make?"

"Well, I'm glad you feel that way."

This time I did help him to the door. He was limping and had broken into a sweat. "You know, my boy, Ned, I'm not very well. That's all right. The old have to make way for the new." He glanced up at the sky and I followed his gaze, to the blue moon.

Was he dying then? Was it imminent?

"Goodnight, Ned," he said. "Someday I'll tell you about my Ned. You wouldn't mind, would you?"

What was this? A "You don't mind indulging a tired old man" routine? Probably. The funny thing was I didn't mind. If he needed to get something off his chest, I was there and told him so. He looked grateful as he let himself into the dark foyer and closed the door behind him. I heard his cough, loud and echoing through the door, as I made my way down the front steps.

That night as soon as we hit the bedroom, Scott said happily, "Let's fuck."

Oh, God, we did, on that night of the blue moon, we fucked all the way till morning and beyond, Sunday morning, when the sounds of distant church bells mixed with the sounds of the surf crashing unseen onto nearby Two Mile Hollow Beach.

THE FOLLOWING FRIDAY I phoned Warren. He hadn't given me a phone number, I suspected because he didn't have his own phone, so I googled the White Pages for the Labotte number. When I called it, he picked up right away, happy to hear my voice. I'd promised to listen to him talk about Ned, but I didn't bring that up, I didn't want to be so obvious. I just asked if he'd like to take a drive to Sag Harbor for lunch. We could meet up with Scott if he liked, and Kevin. He thought that would be fine.

It was about an hour's drive to the North Shore, there were no direct roads, only country lanes. I thought Warren might bring up Ned but he didn't. He just pointed out familiar places along the way, ponds, woods, and even some houses, rustic and weatherbeaten, he remembered as a teenager when he'd drive up from the South Shore.

Once we reached Sag Harbor, I drove to Kevin's subtly majestic Tudor in the middle of town. Scott had phoned me more than once as I approached to let me know he was ready to leave the office to meet us there, but when I pulled into Kevin's driveway he sent me a text. He couldn't get away after all, sorry. "Scott can't make it," I informed Warren as Sam came running out of the house with a birthday hat on and sparklers in her hands. She ran up to the car and breathlessly informed me that she'd gotten that iPad Air as a present, it was better than she ever imagined it would be. Wouldn't we come in and join her party? That's when Kevin appeared on the porch, surrounded by Sam's friends. He waved in our direction but didn't invite us in, only motioned for Sam to come back to the house. "Scott cancelled!" he yelled to us and raised his shoulders in confusion. "I know. It doesn't matter," I called out the window, "Enjoy the celebration!"

As I started to pull away, I watched Kevin gather the kids together to snap some pictures.

"What's he doing?" Warren asked.

"Taking some birthday photos."

"But he doesn't have a camera."

"He's taking them with his phone."

Warren stiffened but smiled.

I drove down to the pier but it wasn't much, just a concrete walkway with cars parked on either side of it all the way to the end where it dropped off into the bay. It wasn't that interesting a spot so I was glad when Warren said he didn't want to stop there, the pier was too full of memories. I wondered what kind. Had he taken a bundle of books with him as a teenager and sat there on a bench all day, reading and daydreaming ... and now that he was old ... possibly near the end of his life ... he didn't want to remember or dwell on it ... *"The old must make way for the new,"* he'd said. He wasn't hungry so I suggested we head home rather than have lunch. The road was winding and empty. When at one point we passed a large woods full of Red and Scarlet oaks, towering like nature's royalty above the hills and dales and over any signs of civilization, Warren asked me to pull over to the side of the road. After I parked there, Warren put his finger gently on my neck. "Your sunburn," he asked, "does it still hurt?"

"No," I said, uncomfortable at his intimate gesture. I don't know why, the old guy wasn't making a pass at me. It was something else. "Scott rubbed cream on it last night. It'll get to the peeling stage soon."

"Scott ... you mean Mr. Farrough. Did you take his last name?"

I smelled the dryness of the earth, it hadn't rained for weeks, and I watched the leaves of the most majestic of the Scarlet oaks blow gently in the breeze.

"Yes."

"So you're Ned Farrough."

I gave him a questioning look but he was expressionless. "That's right ... I'm Ned Farrough."

Suddenly that twinkle was back, the same twinkle he'd had when he'd wiped sugar from that doughnut off his face, a conspiratorial sweetness that only babies and the elderly can pull off with any authenticity. He insisted on taking me into the woods to show me something. It wasn't easy going for him, there was much huffing and puffing and resting against one tree then another, until he brought me into a particularly shady grove, a dark hollow, surrounded by pine trees.

"Here," he said, tapping one of the trees. "Have a look."

There was a heart with the names Warren and Ned carved into the bark, an arrow shot through it.

"We carved it together almost fifty years ago. And it's still here."

Encouragingly, I said, "And will be here for the next hundred too."

"Will it? Do trees live that long?"

"Pines do, they can live a thousand years, some of them."

"Well, then, it's a fitting memorial for us, Ned and me. Lasting longer than our lives, lasting longer than our love."

So. It was time. Warren told me about Ned, how as teenagers they had searched for and found this faraway spot, a hideaway to make their very own, where they could "do it," he said, away from the world's prying eyes. Later they'd deserted these woods to continue their relationship indoors, up until the day Ned died fifteen years ago. Ned had lived in Hampton Bays, a more rough-and-tumble, low-rent version of the Hampton towns proper. He'd owned a grocery store there and lived above it. After they met, to pull the wool over both of their families' eyes, he'd hired Warren as his clerk, his helper. During the day, Warren would work alongside Ned, drive home to his family for dinner, then return to his own studio apartment behind Ned's grocery—and sneak into the grocery through the back way and up the stairs where he and Ned slept in each other's arms. Hidden away, like someone's riches under the floorboards, always afraid of being discovered. And they never were. They played the game too well. Ned had a "beard" in town, a lesbian; they were always seen together, at family affairs, movies, the beach. Warren was just the perennial bachelor. No one had been able to catch him with "dirty hands," he claimed. The worst was after Ned died, bringing this double life to an end, leaving no trace of it for anyone to find. Their love had been real, of course, not a fantasy, he insisted, but still they had been half ghost, half human, only half living and in the end, half dying, Ned fifteen years ago, and Warren ...

I heard a crunch of leaves and imagined Ned's footsteps coming up behind us, but when I turned around it was only a chipmunk.

I sighed.

"No one ever found out about us," Warren said. "We considered that a great victory."

It seemed unbearable, and unbearably sad, an inversion of a victory, a moral catastrophe. The only saving grace, the only light that had shone through was that they had shared this love throughout their lives, even if they'd had to pervert it for the world's sake.

"This carved heart is all that's left of us," Warren confided as he tapped the bark. "The grocery store was sold right after Ned died and bulldozed a few months later to make way for a bunch of condos." He laughed. "The condos have ocean views, I'm told, something we never had."

"No, well, we don't have a view of the ocean either," I added, hoping it would bring us down to a more level playing field. But it didn't, I was Mr. Farrough—and both man and God knew it.

"I said I wanted to tell you about my Ned and you listened to me. I've never told anyone about us before."

"It's always good to hear a love story and yours was one. How did you two meet?"

"On the pier back there. We cruised each other in the men's room. At the urinal."

"Oh." I was a little unnerved but recovered quickly. "Nothing wrong with that. The same thing goes on today. I mean people meet online in chat rooms ... on sex sites ..."

"Is that so?" He paused. "Well, in our day it was the toilets, I'm afraid. Doesn't matter, though, does it? Love is love."

"It certainly is."

"How did you and ... Mr. Farrough meet?"

"Through mutual friends ... at a wedding for another couple ... one groom was a friend of mine and one groom was a friend of Scott's ... and one thing led to another ... I know, it sounds like a sitcom, doesn't it?"

"It does. You're one of the kindest people I've ever met, I just want you to know that."

It was a nice compliment and he may have meant it, although it didn't sound like he'd ever had a big social circle of kind people to choose from. I put one arm around his shoulder, helped him as he hobbled his way to the car, and drove him home.

It was a few days later that Scott told me Kevin and Sam had been the latest victims of one of those curious break-ins. While they were at the movies, the vandal(s) had struck again. They'd dismantled the security system, broken the glass in the kitchen door, unlocked it from the outside, and walked right in. They'd not only gone for Sam's new iPad Air, but all the computers and electronics in the house, pulverizing them to smithereens with something the strength of a sledgehammer. Kevin was really upset. Did they plan to come back again? And who were they?

Scott and I immediately invited Kevin and Sam to stay with us but they declined. Kevin bought a guard dog instead.

"How crazy is that?" I asked Scott as I went out to do battle with my snap beans, wilting on this humid afternoon. "For this to happen to people we know. After we were just talking about these break-ins not that long ago."

"It's pretty crazy. No, it's very fucked." He added, "Remember I told you to be on your guard when I'm at work. That still goes, only double."

"Scott, don't make this into a big drama."

"What do you mean?"

"Nothing. Forget it."

A week passed and August came and we put it out of our minds.

One night, though, I had a dream, I was walking in a strange town, through dark streets with rundown storefronts and boarded-up houses and every now and then I passed a brightly lit filling station that infused the surrounding landscape with color, but soon I was heading back into the tawdry urban amalgamation of blackish houses and crumbling shops. Eventually I was putting my key into the lock of a heavy door and letting myself into a dimly lit room full of cobwebs, and of shelves and shelves stocked with dusty canned goods. I found myself behind the counter of this grocery store, methodically taking can after can down and stacking them on the counter only to have them disappear in thin air. Then I'd methodically replace them with more cans from the plentiful stock on the shelves behind me. *"Aren't you coming to bed yet?"* came a voice from upstairs. *"Oh, God, there are so many customers still to serve,"* I mumbled to myself. Then suddenly a creaky staircase appeared before me. A shadow flickered across the top of it. *"Aren't you coming to bed* yet?" the voice repeated. *"Who are you?"* I asked. *"It's Ned. You know who I am."* *"Ned?"* *"Yes ..."* Oh, of course, the nightly ritual, the nightly ruse. Our secret. *"I'm coming ..."* I wiped my hands on the apron tied around my waist and approached the stairs but I froze at the bottom, filled with dread. *"I'm waiting ..."* came the voice. I opened my mouth to answer but couldn't speak ... *"I'm waiting ..."*

"Honey, you're whimpering, stop it." It was Scott, both comforting me and reproaching me because I'd wakened him at five in the morning. He was the type who couldn't fall back asleep once he was up. "Sorry," I said. "It's not my fault."

"No," he answered. "But why do you have these bad dreams?"

"Do I have them a lot?"

"Only lately, but it seems to me you've had them every night for the past week." The warm summer dawn coming into the room was more than welcomed by me; I wrapped myself in its slowly increasing light and clarity.

Scott and Kevin were peas in a pod. They jogged together, wearing heart monitors and forcing each other into more and more intense fitness challenges, the Zone 5 stuff, passing their lactose thresholds and racing into what new territories? Places I didn't want to go. I worried about Scott whose recovery periods were brutal and long. Maybe I should have worried about something else, the two of them sexing it up on the sly, they were together so much, together alone that is. Right now they were supposed to be running side by side through the bucolic streets of our East Hampton neighborhood, but what did I know, I was on Main Street shopping and taking in some galleries. It's funny. I was never worried about Scott being unfaithful with Kevin or anybody else, like his gym rat buddies for instance. As good looking as he was, he was Mr. Straight Arrow, craving the conventionalities of a married life, concentrating on making money and being respected in his firm. It's also funny because the conventional facade at his firm was just that—all of his peers were sleeping around, I'd heard rumors, and either hiding it or bragging about it, and the gym rats were too, of course. But Scott, he had blinders on, and pretended it was all picket fences, faithfulness, eventual fatherhood, and a narrow road. I would have been more likely to cheat, anybody would have been. But how long would his zealousness for fidelity, duty, and obligation to his ideals last? I'd heard that when that type of man falls, he falls really hard, and not only his world but everybody else's around him goes off orbit. But maybe Scott would never fall from that grace he'd invented. A few men, dare I say, never did.

I made a pit stop into our town grocery and who was there but Warren, this time not indulging in jelly doughnuts, but gulping at a cup of tea and looking wan, disheveled.

"Hello, Warren, I haven't seen you in town. Where have you been keeping yourself?"

"I've been in Southampton Hospital on I.V. for a week."

"Oh, no," I said. "Is there something I can do?"

He sighed. "There's no cure for what I've got."

It was awkward standing there waiting for him to elaborate so when he didn't, I started to leave, expressing my condolences. As I walked out the door, he called after me in a hoarse voice, "I've got Powassan, Ned." I turned back briefly to look at him. "But don't worry, it's not catching, you couldn't pick it up from me."

"No," I said. "Well, I'll be in touch."

Powassan, powassen, powassin, I said it over and over to myself. The first thing I did was walk to the Hampton Jitney bus stop and sit on the bench and google it. The Powassan virus was caused by a rare and deadly tick bite and there was no cure, like Warren said. It brought on every piece of crap symptom under the sun, vomiting, headaches, seizures, memory loss, and caused respiratory problems or swelling in the brain that eventually did you in. Intravenous treatments were required to bring down the swelling in the brain. That's what Warren had been given in Southampton Hospital. So was he in the last stage of this thing? Was that what he was telling me? Jesus Christ, one little tick crawling up your leg. I read on. Ticks that carried the Powassan virus were found in the northeast, of course. Since I gardened, I figured I'd better keep pulling up weeds and see that the grass was cut and wear light-colored clothes and use bug spray. And that went for Scott too.

I had that same dream again several times over the next week. At the end of it, each time I was left not knowing who was calling me from the top of the stairs, although he identified himself as Ned. I had the feeling I never wanted to find out. Sometimes I woke Scott up, whimpering again, and sometimes I didn't, because he wasn't there. On two mornings I found him asleep in the guest bedroom, covers pulled up tight, looking like an angel. And then I felt terrible for disturbing him. I'd close the door and let him sleep a little longer while I made him breakfast.

I also checked in on Warren over the phone now and then. He put on a brave front but he couldn't stifle that racking cough and during one of our conversations admitted that maybe he should give up the ghost. "What do I have to live for anyway?" he asked bluntly.

"That's not the best question to ask yourself right now. You need company, you're too isolated." I insisted he come over and join us for a Saturday morning brunch, Kevin and Sam would be there, and Willie, too, that pharmacist Kevin had been interested in and was dating now. Scott would make Mimosas and I'd try my hand at some corn pancakes with fresh whipped goat cheese. How did that sound? Even as I extended the invitation, I knew it was the wrong thing to do, that no good could come of it, but I did it anyway, I didn't know how not to be nice.

We sat in the kitchen at the big cherrywood table that had plenty of room for the six of us and could have easily accommodated more. I sat between Warren and Scott. We faced Kevin, Sam, and Willie, across the table. It had all started promisingly enough. It turned out Willie, a sweet guy with red hair and freckles, was a frustrated thespian who spun lines from famous plays over and over in his head while he filled prescriptions. At our breakfast he left the mundane world of the pharmacy behind and transformed himself into a cheerful Puck, emoting his way through the soliloquy, *I Am the Merry Wanderer of the Night*. When he got to the lines, "And sometimes lurk I in gossip's bowl, in very likeness of a roasted crab," he madly searched his plate of pancakes for an imaginary crab, prompting Sam to put down her new, replacement iPad Air, which she'd brought along to show Scott, and dissolve into a paroxysm of laughter. Warren started coughing. Scott grimaced and Warren noticed.

"I like you," Sam told Willie. "Don't you like him too, Dad?"

Kevin said, "I thought I did until now. To be honest, I can't follow these old lines. Shakespeare, right? It's not something I'd like to hear before bed." Scott laughed.

Warren coughed again.

Scott said, "For God's sake, man, can't you cover your mouth with a napkin?"

"Scott!" I cried.

"Well, can't he?" my husband asked.

Warren mumbled an apology and sat there chastised. Not knowing what else to do, I got up to clear the table, hoping a little movement would prove a distraction for everybody. Kevin did some scrambling too. In an eager voice, he told Willie about how he'd always wanted to see the Galapagos Islands and now Sam did too. Did he have any interest? Scott nonchalantly brought out his iPhone and stared into its screen. "You know," he observed, "most people think the apps on an iPhone can't be infected with malware, but who are they kidding? They most certainly can. Malware, adware, spyware, you name it. But the thing I hate most is how our phone conversations can be recorded and sent to the attackers. So much for smartphones. That's screwed up, yes?" Looking directly at Warren, he asked, "Anybody know the best way to uninstall malicious apps should the worst happen?"

I turned around in time to see Warren turning red. "I think it's obvious I don't know what you're talking about," he said nervously. "You could be speaking Martian as far as I'm concerned."

"Martian?"

"Did it occur to you that not everybody has an interest in those ridiculous little gadgets that seem to hold such a bizarre fascination for you?"

Scott acted offended. "Excuse me."

"And that goes for everybody else." Warren shot a glance at the others around the table.

"Scott," I said. "Come out back with me for a minute, I need your help with something."

I invited the guests to go relax in the living room while I led Scott out the back door into a brilliant August day full of sunshine and a blustery breeze fresh off the ocean.

"Yes?" Scott asked.

"Scott, you're winding him up on purpose," I blurted. "Just stop it."

"Where did you get an idea like that?"

"He's old and set in his ways. Don't belittle him."

Scott shrugged. "He doesn't seem as helpless and in need of your protection as you think."

I raised my voice. "He's dying. I told you. Can't you get that through your head?"

"Did you call Southampton Hospital to check if he was even a patient there?"

I grabbed his arm. "I don't need to. I only have to look at him to know."

"You told me he was bitten by a tick. Are you sure it wasn't the other way around?"

"Keep your voice down."

"If he's as sick as you say, why does the old motherfucker have to cough in my face, huh?"

Just then I noticed Warren on the back steps watching us arguing on the lawn. "Ned, would you mind taking me back home now?" he asked. "I don't feel well."

"Of course I will, go get in the car."

"Goodbye, Scott," Warren said. "Thanks for everything."

"Take care of yourself then," Scott replied.

Warren pretended to sleep on the short drive home and the only words he said were when I helped him up to the door. He patted me on the shoulder and observed, "You do look out for me, don't you?"

"Yes, I guess I do."

When I got home, I found the group of them quietly sitting around the kitchen table, Scott, Kevin, Willie, and Sam. It was Sam who spoke up, "He's the man who broke into our house."

"What?"

"I just know it was. I know it was him."

I didn't admit it but I'd had that same crazy thought pass through my head once too, shortly after I'd met him, on the afternoon I was pulling up weeds in our garden, only because he wasn't tech savvy and seemed to hold the whole technology boom in contempt. But since I'd gotten to know him better, gotten to know him well, I found the idea completely preposterous. There were plenty of people like him, especially older folks, who lashed out at computers and electronics in general because they didn't know how to use them and simply feared what they didn't understand.

"That's a bit of a stretch," I replied good-naturedly. "Especially since he's old and ill, can hardly walk without stopping to catch his breath, has no car, and no interest in causing anybody harm. I can vouch for that."

"He's the one," Sam insisted.

THE FOLLOWING SUNDAY MORNING, Scott and I arrived at an empty Two Mile Hollow Beach at five-thirty in the morning to watch the sun rise. It had been my idea to set the clock and leave the house when it was still dark, though he'd readily agreed. We lay on blankets anticipating and finally seeing that eruption of a coral orb over the thin-lined horizon. It transformed itself into an orange fireball and sent its rays over the choppy waves toward us. It seemed both supernatural and spiritual, this rising, giving mankind just what it needed but no more.

"If the sun was any hotter," I mused, "we'd burn to a crisp. Any stronger light and we'd be blind."

"When I married you," he said, "I knew I was marrying one of a kind. A poet, a dreamer, a thinker, though I don't know if your thoughts are always right."

"You're full of regrets now?"

"Hardly."

As I ran the sand through my hands, I noticed it was still cold to the touch. I never wanted Scott to get cold to my touch. I worried that I'd gone too far complaining about his treatment of Warren. It would be stupid to have a rift over that.

"I love you," I said.

"I love you," he answered. "But you're like a child in many ways, I need to take care of you."

I had no idea why he said that, I bristled at first, silently, but accepted his assessment. If that was what he honestly thought, what could I do about it? One day when we had kids of our own, my practical side would rise to the fore and he'd see how well I managed to hold up my end of their upbringing. I wondered if it would be long in coming, the time of And Baby Makes Three. In a way, I wanted it to be a long way off, I wanted an endless honeymoon, just him and me. I glanced down at the wedding ring on my finger; I wished I'd left it at home. You never took a wedding ring to a beach. My mom had lost hers in this same Atlantic Ocean, not long after she was married. She'd gone in for a swim with the ring on her finger and had waded to shore to find it gone; it had probably drifted down to Florida or South America, was on the finger of some lucky girl in Miami or Rio, or buried under sand on the bottom of the ocean. That's what happened to all of us as well. Like a wedding ring, we either stayed attached to the guy we married, or drifted from man to man, swept along by strong currents of love or hate until we disappeared from sight, forgotten by everybody. Even God.

Why had I thought that? Because of what had happened to Warren and his Ned? Ned had been taken from Warren in secrecy, a black cloak descending to wrap him in its folds in the dead of night ... then he was gone and his bed left empty. Ned vanished from the world before it had the chance to acknowledge his and Warren's love for each other. I wasn't sure what my relationship with God was, if I even had one, or if I'd develop one down the road, but I didn't think God would be inclined to forget about me, or forget about anyone. Weren't the drifting currents supposed to land us all on some safe shore? Ned, the other Ned, might be waiting on that safe shore now ... *"I'm waiting ... I'm waiting ..."*

Scott and I had made love here, back in the dunes, during the same week we'd moved into our new house. We'd negotiated hot sand, painful thistles, and curious stares until we found a spot hidden by some brush and pines, our hideaway, and we'd had sex, devoured each other with a majestic hunger, then lay there laughing afterwards, our spent cum drying on our bodies with the help of our friend the sun and a rippling, satiating breeze. Suddenly I was horny for Scott and was going to suggest we have another go at it back there in the dunes, but before I could, he stood up, restless, and said he wanted to leave, that the beach was a dull place in the early morning, once you'd seen the spectacle of the sunrise. Something was on his mind.

I found out just what it was that afternoon.

He wanted to visit Warren, casually drop in on him at the Labotte home to smooth things over, make sure there were no ill feelings left over from yesterday's brunch. That didn't sound like Scott, exactly. I agreed to drive over there with him but insisted on phoning Warren first to give him fair warning we were on our way. Fine. Fine by Scott, and as it tuned out, fine by Warren. It wasn't fine by me because I wondered if this could end up as another opportunity for an even more incendiary confrontation between the two of them.

Warren was effervescent—for him: he had a spring in his step I'd never seen before, and took great pleasure in showing Scott the house first and then the garden. Scott wasn't interested in the furnishings or decor like I was; his eyes glazed over in boredom while getting "the tour," and what was there to say about the front garden? The roses were near dead, their petals yellowed and falling off.

"Feeling better, Warren?" Scott asked as Warren surveyed the corpses of the white roses.

"Yes." He added, "Poor roses, they're done. Well, I'm feeling slightly better, that is. I can't do jumping jacks or get on my knees to weed the garden." The front lawn had been newly mowed and the mower sat in the middle of a large ring of clipped grass which reminded me of one of those crop circles in the English countryside. "Of course, I can't mow the lawn either. The boys take care of that." He said to Scott pointedly, "I have some days that are better than others."

"I'm glad this is one of your good ones. We've cleared the air then, you and I?" Scott asked him.

"Yes, of course." He shielded his eyes and looked up at the sky. "Another scorcher today. What do you say we have some iced tea in my quarters?" He led us to his sitting room and told us to relax while he went to get the tea. I sat on the couch while Scott paced around the room. The drapes were closed so the room was a little dark and stuffy. Maybe Warren would air it out when he came in from the kitchen.

"He has a lot of books," Scott said, pausing at the desk.

"It's his favorite thing to do, read. It's a comfort for him."

Scott opened one of them.

I lowered my voice. "Well, are you satisfied now? That all's well?"

"He's marked pages in this *Book of Quotations*," Scott said as he flipped through it. He paused on one page and frowned, then called me over. "He's put a stick 'em note next to one of the quotes. Read it."

I did. It read, *"He who makes a beast of himself removes the pain of being human."* It was attributed to Samuel Johnson.

Warren came in with three tall glasses of iced tea and set them on the table by the window. I stood between him and Scott who discreetly closed the book.

"I'll open the window and we'll catch whatever breeze there is." Warren pulled the drapes back and opened the sliding door. His face went white and he started to tremble. We looked out past him to the pool in the back yard and the two boys I'd seen cleaning it the last time I was here, the blond and dark-haired one, built as if they were spawned from Michelangelo's David, were jumping in and out of the pool, performing crude, dangerous stunts like low-life kids high or drunk, and not giving a damn about spewing vulgarities or seeming to care how self-injuring their pranks were. They were also bare ass.

"Makes for quite a show," Scott observed.

First Warren fumed silently then made a noise like a wounded animal. He stormed outside to challenge them, I assumed because they were nude and lewd and high. I was wrong.

"How dare you?" he screamed. "You no good white trash bastards. Get out of here and don't come back."

They broke into druggy laughter.

"Just look around you," Warren chided them. "You haven't cut the grass in the back here for the last couple of weeks. You think you can just finish the front lawn and let the back lawn grow wild and untended?"

"Oh shut up," the blond one said and flipped him the bird while his buddy told him to "Talk normal."

"Talk normal?" Warren raged. "I'll talk normal. It's because you didn't finish cutting the grass back here, even after I reminded you on a number of occasions, that we have ticks. I warned you. But you didn't listen. And now it's too late. I got bit by one of them." He added melodramatically, "And now I'm dying!"

The boys couldn't have cared less and did a nasty naked dance in front of him. "They're high on something," I whispered to Scott. "He'd better be careful."

No sooner had those words come out of my mouth than they came at him, one with a rake and one with a garden hose, thrusting them like Roman soldiers tormenting their quarry in the Coliseum.

Warren retreated, yelling, "That's it, I'm calling the police right now if you don't get out of here this minute."

That seemed to do it. It was their turn to retreat. They said they'd go, adding that Warren was a fat old slut who lay on his back all day long with his legs spread hoping for the Great Dane from next door to come by and give him a fuck. Warren returned to the sitting room, strangely calm and rubbing his hands. "That's done and dusted. They can stay in Hampton Bays from now on and not cross the invisible line into civilization." Hampton Bays, that's where Warren had said Ned was from, that's where the grocery store had been, maybe that's where Warren himself was from. I asked him. Yes, he was, but from the right side of the tracks while the pool boys Geoff and Beau were from the wrong side of town where they were used to hanging with a bad crowd, "hoodlums" involved in all kinds of wrongdoing, "dope fiends" always in trouble with the law. He should have his head examined for having gotten them work in this refined neighborhood. Well, he'd learned his lesson. Back they went now to that wrong side of the tracks.

"Well," Scott said to him, "under the circumstances, you don't mind if we don't stay for tea, do you?"

"What?" Warren asked absentmindedly.

"I think I've had all the thrills I can take for one day," he said.

"Warren, I'm sorry you had to go through all this," I sympathized.

"Ned, just keep supporting me," he urged. "Promise me."

"You can count on that," I said. "I'll be in touch."

Scott drove us home. When I commented on how weird it was that Warren actually seemed to blame those boys for his tick bite, Scott silenced me. "You know that was a set-up, don't you? A performance for our benefit. It was comical."

I was clueless.

Scott went on to explain that Warren was indeed responsible for those break-ins but that he'd sent those two boys out to actually search and destroy all the personal electronics. He stayed at home, safe and snug, looking up sick quotes in his books while he programmed them like robots to do his bidding. He didn't have to be fleet of foot or drive a car to get the job done. He just had to pay those kids enough so they had cash for drugs, party money.

"Oh, God, I don't know, Scott. It's a theory, but that's all it is. It's one theory in a thousand."

"Oh, yes?" he asked. "Remember that quote in the book he'd marked? Wouldn't you give my theory improved odds after reading that?"

I thought back ... *"He who makes a beast of himself removes the pain of being human ..."*

Is that what Warren was doing? Maybe. If so, it was a frightening thought. A frightening thought to ruin a beautiful, cloudless August day, and darken, even overwhelm, the memory of the morning's sunrise.

THE NEXT EVENING WAS dull and gray and it segued slowly and almost imperceptibly into complete darkness. I could hear distant thunder. I checked the weather while I watched Scott in the kitchen, pacing back and forth, talking to somebody on the phone. The weather report called for rain at some point tonight with the chance of a passing severe thunderstorm. We could use the rain. My vegetable garden had faded in the semi-drought, though the constant sun had made for a great month on the beach.

Scott came in from the kitchen and sat down next to me on the sofa and explained he'd been on the phone with Matt Randy, our next door neighbor, who told him an impromptu meeting was in progress at the home of the family over on Egypt Close who'd been vandalized a few weeks ago. A prowler had been spotted last night at the same house, peeping in the windows before making his escape. Matt hadn't been willing to give details over the phone but had suggested there was something more menacing about the situation than the prowler just trying to get a peek inside.

"By the way," Scott said, "Matt said the prowler could have been a teenaged boy and that he could have had an accomplice. That sounds just about right, doesn't it?"

"This whole thing is out of my league," I said cautiously.

Scott said he was going to the meeting and thought I should be there too.

"Oh, no, we both don't need to go," I protested. "You can pass along what you hear to me later—or vice versa, if you'd rather I go."

"Oh, no, I'm definitely going," Scott said. "I'm walking over with Matt. I don't know how long this thing will last, maybe an hour or so. I'll be back by ten."

After Scott left, I went out back and took my flashlight with me since there were heavy clouds preventing any stars or moon to light the way. I walked to the edge of the back lawn to check on my vegetable garden. There was nothing left of it. My black thumb had seen to that. My black thumb and some scavengers, those nocturnal enemies who'd had my vegetables on their greedy radars. I'd try to plant something new in the fall.

I pointed the beam of the flashlight up and down the trees. The wind had picked up and the leaves were blowing hard as they always do before a coming storm. The summer night wind felt good and I pictured Two Mile Hollow Beach and thought how dark and romantic it would be there now. Oh, to have sex in the dunes on a night like this, amid peals of thunder while the waves whipped themselves into a frenzy. Scott was lucky he was at that meeting or I'd have talked him into going there right now. I crossed the lawn and went back inside the house just as raindrops began to fall, big ones splattering down on the back porch. I watched them slide down the kitchen panes for a few minutes but then the rain let up.

I went back into the living room and lay down on the sofa, talking myself into a nap. But just as I closed my eyes I thought I heard a cough from somebody outside on the driveway. It couldn't be, could it?

When I opened the front door, I saw Warren standing still as a statue in the middle of the driveway, bundled up in a long raincoat, staring at me.

"Warren," I called. "Come on in."

He approached the front door hesitantly, then stepped inside. There was anger in his eyes. Uneasy, I shut the door behind him.

"Did you walk all the way over here?" I asked. He nodded.

"Well, let me have your raincoat and I'll make you some tea or coffee." Scott wouldn't approve of this, of Warren taking it into his head to visit us unannounced. Did he think he'd be able to just drop in, whenever he pleased? I'd have to gently disavow him of that.

"I don't want any tea or coffee. And I'll keep my raincoat on. I won't be staying."

"Oh, no? Why did you stop by?"

"Where's your husband?" he asked.

For some reason, I told him Scott was asleep upstairs.

"Well, get him," he ordered angrily.

"No, Warren, he's not feeling well tonight."

"Then I'll tell you. One of you paged through my *Book of Quotations*. You lost my place and made a new crease at the top of one of the pages. A page you'd been looking at."

"I don't know what you're going on about."

"Oh, no?"

"Absolutely not. You walked over here just to tell me that?"

"No," he said. He paused, then asked me slowly, "You think you're better than everybody else, you think you have everything, don't you?"

I looked down, confused.

"And maybe you do," he continued. "By a cruel twist of fate." He coughed. "By being born in a different time."

"Warren, why don't you go home now? You'd be better off."

"Not yet, Ned. I hate that name. Ned. That was the name of the man I lived with all my life, in secret, our relationship hidden from the world."

"I know."

"What do you know? In the eyes of the law you and Mr. Farrough are equal. Equal partners. I spent my life trusting Ned, believing our love would last forever, working for him in that horrible store, sleeping with him every night, worrying about him, taking care of him when he was sick. I was his husband if you ask me."

"I'm sure you were."

"But then things changed. He met another man and dumped me fifteen years ago. He didn't die. The two of them kicked me out and got money for the store from developers and went off to California, to Palm Springs, where they bought a glass house in the desert where nobody dared throw any stones at them, while I was helpless as I watched the grocery store pulled down, a store I didn't own a penny of, and condos built up in the place I'd lain my head. What right did I have to share in any of the store? I was never legally married so I couldn't be divorced. No one had even known I'd had a relationship with Ned, so no one could advise me. I had lived off the whims of another man nobody knew existed, with nothing to show for it in the end. I was left destitute, a man over fifty who'd never had a job except to slave for my lover. I had to beg for handouts until I was lucky enough to get a caretaker position with old Mrs. Labotte. I'll die in her house, with nothing to call my own, no man, no money, no sympathy. Do you wonder that I'm bitter, that I made myself into a beast to remove the pain of being human?"

"I'm sorry."

"But I don't need to tell you that. You found that out already, didn't you, you and Scott together, by prying, by unmasking the one secret I still had, the one embarrassing thing that defines me. The two of you have robbed me of what was left of my dignity just as much as Ned did. In fact, you are Ned. You're the second Ned come to blight my life and somehow there will be a judgment day for you as surely as there was for me. No matter that you have the law on your side today and the sun shining on your head."

At that, he turned and left, limping back down the driveway. I shut the door behind him and leaned back against it, shaking, feeling like I'd sustained a number of savage body blows, but I hadn't. I'd only had a tongue-lashing, heard a malediction from an old man full of resentment. I could tell myself it didn't matter, but I was devastated.

Suddenly my phone rang. I could see it was Scott calling. "Yes?" I said anxiously.

"Ned. I have to tell you, things are worse than they let on. This kid, this teenager, he wore a mask, one of those white hockey masks, you know a goalie mask that looks like something out of *Friday the 13th*. His blond hair was sticking out above it, that's how I know it was one of Warren's boys. That, and another reason. When he crept up on the house here on Egypt Close, he had a big, ugly gnarled club in his hand and he broke into the house swinging it, just the way that blond kid swung that rake at Warren yesterday. The owner scared him off with his gun."

"That was lucky."

"I don't want to alarm you, but somebody spotted him tonight, hanging around a house on our street."

"What are you saying?"

"He's out there in that same hockey mask and carrying that big club. I called the cops. I'm coming back now, but I want you to go upstairs and get the gun. You know where it is, in the box on the top shelf of the closet, right?"

"Oh, no, Scott," I said, trembling, "with a gun you're asking for trouble, for something bad to happen. Just hurry home."

"Go get the gun." A loud peal of thunder shook the house down to its foundation and the windows rattled. It was followed by a flash of lightning that lit the room like an explosion. "You can't afford not to. Just do what I tell you." He hung up.

Suddenly the house went dark. There was no power. And no Scott. It was just me alone.

I heard the sound of light rain on the roof, surprised that it wasn't a downpour given the violence of the thunder and lightning, but it wasn't. It was a quiet rain, deceptive. I closed my eyes, immobilized.

Then I started to let my imagination run to dark places. The first floor of the house was full of windows. It was ridiculous, but windows that normally provided a much welcome view out into the world suddenly turned, in a moment of panic, into funhouse mirrors, crazy glass, ready to distort any man on the other side into a monster.

From the murky kitchen, I watched a flash of lightning illuminate the yard and the silhouettes of the black trees, but nothing else, no hiding figure, no creeping shadow among them.

But still I felt sick. I made my way up the stairs, feeling a cold and clammy imaginary breath on the back of my neck.

I got the gun from the box on the closet shelf. I'd been trained to shoot a gun when I was twelve by my uncle. He owned a firing range and was a great marksman. After Scott and I spent a day shooting with him on the range, he claimed I was a better shot than Scott. But how did that help me now? The problem was I was more fragile than Scott. More the poet, like Scott had told me on the beach. I just wanted to shut myself in the bedroom until my husband got home. And I did.

Until the idea occurred to me that someone could already be in the house. In my mind, I pictured an intruder surreptitiously climbing up the stairs while I waited in false security behind an unlocked wooden door. That scenario was more than I could bear, one that left me feeling like a sitting duck. Cautiously I made my way back downstairs.

I sat at the dining room table, in the dark, the gun held out in front of me, one eye on the window that faced the back yard and the other on the dining room door. It seemed I waited forever in a netherworld for something to happen. I started sweating and felt my muscles spasm. Then in a brief flash of lightning I saw the boy in the hockey mask standing in the middle of the back yard, holding the club. I jumped up. Scott was right. He was the blond boy from the pool at Warren's, without a doubt it was him. Slowly I backed away from the window toward the dining room door, the gun still held out in front of me. Then I made a swift turn into the living room. That's when he came at me from around the corner, from inside the kitchen. Another bolt of lightning showed his white mask and blond hair. I screamed as I shot him.

I WAS A KILLER, but I wasn't a murderer, there's a huge difference. Though not to some, for them the lines were blurred. Kevin, Sam, and Willy cut off all relations with me, unsure of the truth, while Scott's family, naturally, rejected me as well, not even caring what the truth was. They pushed the Suffolk County D.A. to charge me with murder in their son's death.

The East Hampton town police arrested me that stormy August night for shooting Scott and held me in the town jail while they tried to figure out what to charge me with. In the end they let me go and have let me alone since, due mainly to that phone call made to them by Scott himself, warning them a prowler was in the area, and also by the subsequent capture and arrest of that prowler, Geoff Lang, for intent to break and enter, among other crimes. As far as I was concerned, this was over. But the D.A. wasn't willing to rule Scott's death as accidental just yet, they were still trying to see if there wasn't a crime they could accuse and convict me of.

But I knew there wasn't. It had been Geoff Lang I'd seen in the yard in that flash of lightning, a menacing figure in a hockey goalie mask, holding a gnarled club. Yet the man who'd rushed toward me from the kitchen had been Scott, hurrying into the house to make sure I was all right. He had the same blond hair as Geoff and the same physique; I'd thought he'd been wearing a mask, but it was because his face had taken on a white glow in the shadowy, gray light. Geoff was the man I thought I'd shot in a moment of panic.

It turned out that Geoff and his dark-haired buddy Beau, the boys Warren had hired to tend the Labottes' grounds, had been part of a teenaged gang from the lower-class section of Hampton Bays. My lawyer told me they had a clubhouse where they performed dark rituals, cut themselves with knives and mingled their blood, and took lots of crystal meth. I don't know if all of that was true or if my lawyer was just trying to help my case, but they were responsible for the break-ins in the Springs and East Hampton, and the media ran with the cult angle.

Apparently the gang members forced each other into dangerous rituals to prove their loyalty, to prove they were bad-asses. One of their rituals was to vandalize homes, but only in wealthy neighborhoods, it was more of a kick, and the rich bastards deserved it. Their game was to break the electronics since that was what the vandals themselves valued most and they figured their owners must as well. Geoff and Beau learned about the streets and the homes and the routines of the residents during the time they worked at the Labottes. After their break-ins, they got off reading about their exploits online, but as their drug use escalated, they lost control and decided to ratchet it up a notch, starting to terrify the residents by popping up in scary masks and carrying sticks and clubs that could be used as deadly weapons.

The irony in this was that Warren had nothing to do with any of it, didn't know what the boys were up to, although I could imagine him smiling to himself each time he heard about some electronics item being destroyed. It seemed all he was concerned about was his tick bite and his everlasting bitterness at being left behind in the world by his lover, at being discarded like an old typewriter for something new and shiny.

It's a terrible thing to admit but I didn't feel like this was the end of the world. I in no way blamed myself for Scott's death and he wouldn't have blamed me either. It was a cosmic mistake, almost like a tornado or hurricane, an act of God. I was young and had my life ahead of me. I didn't want to spend it mired in guilt or live a life of regret like Warren had. I didn't deserve it. I'd always been a good person, lending a hand to anyone who needed it, trying to make Scott's life as happy as I could. I wasn't going to turn into the beast Warren embraced, the beast who hated all of mankind. Speaking of Warren, I passed him on Main Street the other day. He was walking with a woman I assumed could be none other than Mrs. Labotte returned from Europe, in a chic yellow chiffon dress, a chain of small pearls around her neck, her gray hair elegantly coiffed. Warren noticed me and immediately looked down at his feet and coughed for good measure. He might have offered me his condolences. Oh, but he'd turned into that beast, so it wouldn't be possible.

It was odd but I'd stifled my emotions about Scott. I hadn't gone to the funeral, not only because his parents asked me not to, that was the word from their lawyer to mine, but because of the fear that reporters would be there to snap my picture and badger me. Although my fear was off base. My photo had appeared in the news only once, and I'd never caught any reporters hanging around my house or going through the garbage. Matt Randy, from the house next door, told me it was because when the media discovered there hadn't been a crime, they weren't interested. Also he said because I was gay, it made them less interested as well. The public would prefer a juicy story of a wife having an affair with her gardener and shooting her husband in cold blood. The reporters did follow up on the boys though, dug into their cult, their backgrounds, their drug use. That's what scared the residents, Matt insisted, the idea of a Manson-like gang roaming free on the staid, smart streets of East Hampton.

My family reached out to me, insisted I move in with them, told me they understood how impossible it would be for me to stay in the house by myself after what had happened. But I resisted. I preferred being alone, sleeping in the same bed, making meals in the same kitchen, planning some new planting out back. I didn't want to run away from anything. That's not to say I stayed in the house like a recluse. I went on long drives as well. Like the media, I had a fascination with the Hampton Bays Boys as they were called and drove there to look for signs of them, to see if they really had a clubhouse, to get a glimpse of the wrong side of the tracks. But I never found them or the wrong side of the tracks. I did see a big condo with balconies that had views of the Atlantic and instinctively I knew that was the spot where Ned's grocery store had stood. It was odd, to see the condo dwellers out relaxing on their balconies, knowing Warren was going over a list of duties for Mrs. Labotte at her house a few streets over from mine.

After my excursion into Hampton Bays, I preferred to drive east, not west, to places I wasn't familiar with, to the towns and beaches of Amagansett and Montauk. I didn't go back to the gay beach at Two Mile Hollow or drive up to Sag Harbor. I wanted something different. And that's what I did, from the end of the summer into the fall, into October when the air was crisp, even cold, and the leaves had turned a hundred different shades, or so it seemed. I was on the lookout for new adventures.

One afternoon I drove to the open market in Amagansett and strolled in the garden, checking out the chrysanthemums. And the plump new pumpkins. A tall guy next to me asked which one I liked. I answered quickly that I didn't know. Then he picked a big pumpkin out for himself and asked me if I'd help him carve it. I laughed then took a good look at him. He was gorgeous, square-jawed, with purple black hair and violet eyes. He couldn't have been more than thirty. My heart skipped a beat.

"At least help me carry it to my car," he insisted, which I did, the two of us on either side of the monster pumpkin. We slid it onto his back seat, then he asked me to sit with him awhile in his car. I slid onto the passenger seat.

"You do have to help me carve it, you know," he insisted. I swallowed hard at the thought. His name was Clay and he lived on Amagansett Bay. He was an interior designer hired by rich Hampton residents and had been living out here two years now. He was pleasant, really easy to get along with. And sexy as hell. I could have listened to him talk all day. But when he asked about me, I froze. Had he already seen my photo in connection with the shooting? Did he recognize me? I realized I had a secret, something to hide, and when it was revealed to him, would it matter, yes or no? In the end I couldn't mumble anything except that I was from East Hampton. When he asked what street I lived on, I shrugged. He smiled and assured me I'd have plenty of time to tell him. Awkwardly, I looked down at the wedding ring around my finger and hid my hand between my knees. With the other hand, I managed to get the ring off. My mother. Losing her ring in the Atlantic. It drifted down to Miami or Rio. Like a wedding ring, we either stayed attached to the man we married or drifted ...

A few raindrops started falling on his windshield. He asked me if I'd like to follow him home in my car. I just stared at the rain as he turned on his wipers.

"Come on back," he urged. "It's going to be a rainy night. I'll build a fire."

Well, why not? "I'm up for it," I agreed.

"Right answer." He squeezed my leg. "You won't be sorry."

"No, I can't," I said, surprising myself.

He looked crestfallen, honestly crestfallen, which made me wish I'd said yes. "You aren't going to help me carve my pumpkin? You're going to leave me now?"

"Yes, but I will help carve your pumpkin ... only another night."

Did he think I was a skittish virgin or playing games with him? I sighed as I inputted his number on my phone and told him I'd call. There was something ridiculous about me not giving him mine, but I couldn't, not yet. He didn't press me. It was time for me to get out of his car so he could drive home, but I didn't want to. I did though, reluctantly. But not before giving him a deep kiss and experiencing the pleasure of him kissing me back.

From the front seat of my car, I watched him drive off, his taillights disappearing from view in the rain, heading back to his cozy house on Amagansett Bay, a man who needed help with carving a pumpkin and somebody to make love to.

That night I had that dream again. I hadn't had it in a long time. I came into the store by the back way, making sure nobody saw me. Then I started my task of taking dusty canned goods down from the shelf and lining them up on the counter. *"Aren't you coming up to bed yet?"* came a voice from upstairs. *"Oh, God, there are so many customers ..."* A shadow flickered across the top of the creaky staircase. *"Aren't you coming up to bed yet?"* the voice repeated. *"Who are you?"* I asked. *"It's Ned. You know who I am."* *"Ned?"* *"Yes ..."* Oh, of course, the nightly ritual, the nightly ruse. Our secret. *"I'm coming ..."* I wiped my hands on the apron tied around my waist and approached the stairs but I froze at the bottom, filled with dread. *"I'm waiting ..."* came the voice. I opened my mouth to answer but couldn't speak. *"I'm waiting ..."* Then he appeared at the top of those stairs. It was Scott with his face terribly injured from the gunshot wound, and his mouth full of blood, the way I'd left him. I was finally seeing the face I hadn't been able to look at before.

I sobbed for hours, deep heaving sobs from the depths of my gut. I missed Scott so much. I was so, so sorry. Oh, dear God.

THE NEXT AFTERNOON I was out back gardening when my lawyer came by to see me. He cast his shadow over the lawn much as I remembered Scott's shadow elongated over the rippling summer grass. Only my lawyer's shadow wasn't very imposing and the ground was cold, the best for planting spring bulbs. I'd decided not to try any more vegetables, but plant flowers, English bluebells and daffodils, ready to bloom in spring.

"I'm purposely planting bulbs that deer and other critters don't like to nibble. Not that we have any deer," I said. "And plants that need a period of cold before they bloom."

"Ned," my lawyer said gravely, "I have some unsettling news to share with you. You're going to be charged with second degree murder, although I'll do my best to get the charges reduced to manslaughter."

I quietly wiped my face with the back of my hand. "Oh, how come?"

It seemed, according to my lawyer, that the cops had canvassed all the neighbors asking them about Scott and me, encouraging them to comment on our relationship. One of them, a guy named Warren, swore that Scott and I didn't get along. He remembered in particular a terrible quarrel Scott and I had after a brunch we'd asked him to. Warren said he'd had to come out into the back yard to break up a fight Scott and I were having over our computers and personal electronics of all things. He'd been afraid I was going to get violent and attack Scott and he'd stopped me just in time, throwing himself squarely between us. But he couldn't forget my terrible animosity. On another occasion, Warren claimed I'd dropped by the house and told him I was close to asking Scott for a divorce. Warren agreed to testify in court, but he didn't know much more, after all he was only a neighbor.

"I see," I said. "Well, do your best for me." My lawyer assured me that he would.

"It's a lie, of course," I said. "The man hates me."

My lawyer cleared his throat. "Oh, yes? It's the first I've heard of this."

I shrugged. "It's a long story. One I'll have to figure out if it's worth telling."

He replied evenly, "It's not only worth telling, you'll have to tell it, to counter his false claims."

"Yeah, I guess I will," I said, standing up. "Only right now I have something more important to do." I shook his hand and told him to have a good day and then went inside the house. A few days ago I'd taken off my wedding ring when I was in the car with Clay. I remembered that I'd put it in my pocket and taken it home. But damned if I knew where I'd put it after that. I spent all night, turning the house upside down, looking for it, but I couldn't find it. I never did.

NARCISSIST

Young Compton threw cold water on his face and tucked in his shirt, then devoured the cream of wheat he'd doctored up with some maple syrup.

His dad glared at him over a pair of horn-rimmed glasses. "Heard about an accident over by Holiday Lake. Boy on a motorcycle being a daredevil. Got his leg crushed. That's it. Can't walk now."

"Dad, lose those glasses. They're not hip."

"The boy is crippled for life."

Steven pushed his hair out of his eyes. "So? What's that got to do with me?"

"A hell of a lot. You ought to give that crap up and start thinking about ways you're going to make a living. I'll help you out. You know that."

"Yeah, Dad. Sure, I do. But I'm not ready yet. Let me be my own age."

His mom chimed in, "The problem is that boys your age get hurt. Don't let your friends goad you into doing dumb stunts or tricks. Promise me."

"I promise."

"I don't want to lose you at eighteen."

"You won't."

His dad added, "I bought you that sports bike and it cost me plenty, even second hand. But it's time for you to knuckle down now. You're a senior but you're not even graduating this month with the rest of your class. You have to take an extra semester in the fall. That's because you hang out with a bunch of dopes."

"Don't worry. Making up a couple of classes is no big deal." He finished off his orange juice. "And by the way, I'm not a kid anymore. The Army recruiter who showed up at school said because I'm eighteen I can join the army and don't even need my parents' permission."

"So, you're leaving us now?" his dad asked casually while his mom almost spilled her coffee.

"No. But I can get married, start a family, vote, and join the army if I want. And I can phone in myself now when I need to give an excuse for missing school."

"I imagine you can't wait to try that one out," his dad quipped.

"You've got to stop treating me like a kid. I'm an adult now so trust me to make the right decisions."

THE MOTORCYCLE PATH DEEPENED the dirt road that severed Tim Grey's farmhouse from a grove of Scots pines with their splashy orange bark and long needles. Every day after school a pack of local youths stormed by on their bikes, traveling in a neat line, and today was no different. Tim trembled at the window, watching, marveling at their speed, precision, and virility.

After the sound died away and he was alone, Tim ventured outside and inspected the new ruts formed by the wheels that sent the dust as high as the shingles and sometimes sawed rocks in two. Then he squinched his eyes to find the bikes which seemed like high-strung beetles dancing and shimmering far off where the edges of the cornfield blended with the sky. But harvesting corn was months away. All he could see now were fields of muted color, bare, waiting to spring to life ...

This afternoon the air smelled unusually clean to him, and he lifted his shoulders, sucked in his stomach until his muscles ached, and strode vigorously down the road, having decided to pay a visit to his friend, Kyle Efferham.

Efferham lived by himself in a rambling, almost dirty farmhouse on the outskirts of the small town of Ferdinand in Dubois County in southern Indiana. The population of Ferdinand "only ran close to two thousand, give or take," Efferham claimed, and he avoided that "Big City" as much as he could. His crowd were the farmers out on the outskirts of Ferdinand who liked Efferham and remembered his family who had tilled the land for generations.

Efferham was a true conundrum. A widower, sixty-two years old, miserly, and an inveterate gossip, he was a tobacco-chewing, plain talker who fit in. Still, he'd read almost a hundred volumes of world history, poetry, and the classics, many of which stood on spanking clean shelves while the rest of his place was full of dust. For that reason, he enjoyed his neighbor Tim Grey's visits. He could show off.

TIM HAD FALLEN INTO a pattern.

He usually stopped by Kyle's three or four times a week, in the late afternoon or just before sundown. He and Efferham shared a beer on the porch where they traded tales, though Grey was quiet by nature, and it took Efferham several months to coax the man into opening up.

Efferham was surprised to learn that Grey had been a classics scholar and professor at IU Bloomington. Grey, recently retired, had bought an old farmhouse on the outskirts of Ferdinand where his wife had been born. She'd recently passed away and Tim had brought her home to bury her and then decided to stay on. He was pretty much a loner with his Ancient Greek and Latin texts and academic papers he'd written over the years. But he also enjoyed the companionship of Kyle whose laid-back personality he'd come to appreciate.

The fact of the matter was that Grey had settled comfortably into this rural, solitary life. He started his days over cups of fresh brewed coffee, rereading Chaucer, Rabelais and Balzac, as well as his specialties—the tragedies, comedies and histories of Greek antiquity. Then he'd stare out the window at the grove of Scots pines, the most splendid group of trees in the area. He ventured into town only once a week to buy food and sometimes mail a letter to a niece who lived in Ohio. No quick, impersonal texts for him. The modern world was too vast and complicated these days. Simplicity was all that mattered.

TIM GREY ARRIVED AT Efferham's in the late afternoon, earlier than usual. He guessed he'd been energized by watching those boys speed by on their bikes and was up for a talk with Kyle. Yet after the two shared a few beers, Tim turned melancholy. "Guess I've come here to die too, to be by my wife," Tim insisted to Efferham and laughed nervously.

"What are you talking about? You're just in your early fifties. Hell, I buried my wife some years ago and my son and his family picked up and left for Georgia, but I still got plenty of life left in these old bones." He gave Tim a shrewd look. "Sometimes I get the feeling you ain't never even lived yet."

"Sure I have, Kyle," Tim grinned, then described the happy years he and his wife Cynthia had spent taking their camper all over the U.S. and all the magnificent sights they'd seen. Kyle Efferham scoffed silently as he had never been anywhere and had no desire to leave the farm.

"Shut up about all that," Efferham warned. "Nowhere you've seen can compare to Troy." And he meant Homer's Troy.

Efferham, unworldly and with no formal education, took a volume of *The Iliad* off his shelf and engaged Grey in a discussion about the major conflicts and battles and the principal combatants, then afterwards chewed over his favorite tales from Greek mythology, making Grey relive them with him.

Grey, sighing, admitted to Efferham, "Well, I'm rooted here myself now, just like you, and I'm very content. Very content indeed."

But one spring evening, Tim Grey became restless.

"I'M GOING TO TAKE the bike out," Steven informed his dad who'd just come home from a four-hour sales junket.

"Oh, yes? You're going out and I'm coming in."

"Yep."

"There's some weather up ahead."

Steven ignored his armchair forecast. "You and Mom can have dinner without me."

"Nothing new about that," his mom called in from the kitchen. "Ever since you got your license, you take that thing out all hours of the day and night. If you had an accident ... or if you didn't get hurt yourself, but *caused* an accident—"

"Look, I'm over eighteen."

"So you keep saying," she said.

"That means you and Dad didn't have to sign any agreement of financial liability. It's on me. I'm my own man."

"That's not the point," she said. And then added, "Oh, forget it, Steven."

He was out the door but he could hear her last words to his dad as he bounded down the porch steps. "He's still so young and vulnerable, no matter how he—or the law—sees things. I just know he's at risk of getting hurt and hurt bad. That's just statistics mixed with common sense."

T IM HAD BEEN READING since morning and his eyes burned. He wanted to brew a strong cup of coffee but found he'd almost emptied the can. He knew the grocery on the edge of Ferdinand would be closing about now but if he hurried ...

He wanted a walk anyway, so he headed toward town but after about fifteen minutes he regretted his decision. Dark clouds were forming, and the sound of thunder crackled, distorted, like it was coming out of a radio with poor reception. He'd worn a heavy jacket but no hat. He picked up his pace. He figured he'd be able to reach town in about ten minutes and beat the storm then find shelter under some awning if nothing else. If he turned back now, he'd get drenched.

Grey pressed on, sending twigs flying in the air, that's how crisp and hard his steps were. There wasn't even a tree to protect him now, only open fields spreading like a maize-colored blanket to the small town whose distant lights welcomed him. Frivolous raindrops began to fall but Grey knew the fury waiting behind the facade and broke into a run.

Suddenly there was a buzz which couldn't be mistaken for the strange, fitful thunder he'd heard before. The buzz became deafening, and Grey whipped around to find a black motorcycle bearing down on him. He hopped to the side of the road as it jerked to a halt in front of him.

A teenaged boy with blond hair falling past his shoulders, his face losing light like the countryside, studied him, anxiously revving the motor with his ankle-high boots. Grey, startled, turned his head away.

"Hey!" came the shout from the youth on the bike.

"What?" Grey's tone was clipped.

"You're screwed, dude. You got some ways to go yet."

Grey stared defiantly. "What's a little rain, anyway? It's spring. I'm not likely to catch pneumonia."

"Spring, hell. That rain's gonna be cold, slice you just like ice."

Grey shrugged. This was obviously one of the youths who roared past his place each day, though he'd never had a close look at any of them. But he *had* admired them all from afar. And Grey knew himself well enough to know when he came face to face with something he admired, he froze and pretended disinterest. This time was no different. "Doesn't faze me, I tell you."

The boy cracked a smile and Grey was shocked to see how white and perfect his teeth were, how strong his jaw was.

"I was gonna offer you a ride. Still am. Climb on."

And in a flash, the boy gunned the bike toward town, his back raised, looking like he was astride a pitch-black sable horse, his blond hair streaming behind. Grey crushed his fingers against his temple.

The rain came in earnest now, slanted, Grey couldn't escape it. When he reached the edge of town, he was chilled to the bone. No dry spot on him. The streets were empty, and the grocery was closed. Fortunately, there were lights on in a café, though he had to pound on the window to get the attention of a tired-looking woman who unlocked the door and let him in.

"I was just thinking of closing," she said. "Figured nobody'd be out in this, might as well lock up and go home. But then, here you are. A customer. So, I'm officially still open."

"And *I'm* soaking wet. I don't live in town, by the way, I couldn't get home to dry off."

She laughed, disappeared, and returned with a towel. "Why don't you dry off in the bathroom and then I'll cook you whatever you want."

He glanced out at the harsh rain pummeling the street. An old man ran by with a cardboard box over his head. The rain fell harder yet, and lightning filled the room. Grey took the towel into the bathroom. It took close to five minutes to get his hair dry. Gazing in the mirror, he was surprised at how stringy it was and how thin he looked in his jacket hanging on him as loose as on a storefront dummy. Besides that, it was wet through and through, so he took it off.

He ordered bacon and eggs and drank two cups of coffee. All under the watchful gaze of the woman.

"You don't sell cans of coffee by any chance?" he asked her after he'd finished.

"I'll put some coffee in an empty tin for you to take home ... You're Tim Grey, aren't you?"

Tim stared blankly. "I don't think we've met."

"I'm Hazel Kruger. I was at school with your wife. I even went to your wedding thirty years ago." She brushed a strand of brown hair already turning gray off her forehead. "I know, time flies. I buried my husband seven years ago. This year I finished paying off the mortgage on this place. And saw my daughter married off."

Like Kyle, she had a way of distilling the salient points of her past in a few brisk sentences. "Congratulations."

"It's no fun getting old."

"Tell me about it," Tim commiserated. But he didn't feel old.

"*Older*, I should have said," she corrected herself. "Not old."

Tim didn't feel older either. Not much older than the day when this woman, Hazel Kruger, attended his wedding thirty years ago ... But, of course, he was.

Hazel went into the back and filled an empty can with fresh coffee grounds and made him a present of it. "I couldn't afford a wedding gift for you way back when. So, this will have to make up for it."

"Strong coffee? It more than does."

She laughed and asked Tim how he was adjusting to settling down here, how he spent his days. He got the distinct feeling that she was interested in him as possible husband material. He didn't want to encourage her.

"Well, the rain's stopped," Tim noted. "Better be on my way."

He trudged home through the mud, and exhausted, fell asleep before ten o'clock.

THE NEXT AFTERNOON, GREY was deep into a book about the Greek gods when he heard the bikes approaching his house, the ground rumbling and noise picking up intensity like a freight train. He gazed through the glass—a movie screen on which a vital spark would soon dispel the still life in front of him now. Indeed, the bikes soon raced by in a symmetrical line and Grey searched for the blond boy who'd offered him a ride during last night's storm.

Streaks of brown hair, of red, of gold and black. Finally, bringing up the rear was *his* boy whose flaxen hair put the very light to shame. Grey paused. He was panting and his heart was beating too quickly. Once again, Grey crushed his fingers against his temple.

Grey slumped into his chair, foregoing his usual expedition outside to inspect the wheel tracks.

He remained like that, silent, into the evening, unable to shake off the image of the blond boy. Wherever he looked, the image hovered. Even if he shut his eyes, there was his face from last night, the hair becoming ever lighter in the grip of the storm, his face darkening, his bike rearing up like a jagged stone.

Grey was determined to discover the boy's identity.

He made an unnecessary trip into town, but this time he felt like a schoolboy, footloose and fancy free. He nodded to strangers in the street and joked quietly with the postman, all the while on the lookout for signs of the boy. He ate at the little café which now seemed as familiar as his own kitchen table, though he was only polite, even distant to Hazel.

Afterwards, he walked through a park full of crabapple trees and magnolias and wrought iron benches and he thought he was far away from the world as he knew it, with its internet and mobile phones and constant distractions. Here, it could have been fifty years ago, and nothing would be different. No, longer than fifty years ago … much longer … There was a timelessness about the place. A timelessness that stretched into the past as far as the eye could see and the imagination permitted.

By sundown he was on the edge of town, heading home. A dilapidated house, facing the fields that stretched toward Grey's own farmhouse, caught his eye. But it was the black bike chained beside the porch that made him stop dead in his tracks. He held his breath, listening to some rock anthem bellowing from an upstairs room.

He concealed himself across the road in an abandoned barn and watched the house from between the slats. It wasn't long before the music stopped and the porch door swung open and the boy leaped down the steps two at a time, unchained his bike and walked it right by the spot where Grey was concealed. Grey got to see the boy up close as he peered through the slats. His skin was milky, smooth, and his eyes, bordered by sleepy lashes, were large, oval shaped, and a cheerful warm brown. Light hairs disappeared beneath his T-shirt and broke out again on his wide hands gripping the handles.

Of course, Tim Grey had taught good-looking young men at the university, but being married to Cynthia and in love, he'd never really seen them, only through them. Not this time. He looked directly at this boy, the most stunning figure he'd ever seen.

The boy took off on the bike and Grey raced out of the abandoned barn to watch him speeding through the fields toward the blind orb of the sun and Grey could taste the dust that the wind carried back to him.

He looked around helplessly.

As chance would have it, a woman came out of the house next door and started doing some gardening.

"Excuse me." Tim Grey approached her.

"What do you want, mister? Are you a salesman?"

"No, my name is Tim Grey. I don't live far down the road."

"Oh, yes." She shaded her eyes. "I've heard some gossip about you. From Kyle Efferham. You're a teacher. I knew your wife."

"You, too?"

"What do you mean?"

"Hazel from the café went to school with her."

"So did I. It's a small town."

"Could I ask a question?"

"You can ask me a question as long as you let me plant my autumn amaryllis. I love my showy red flowers coming in on the tail end of summer and I'm not going to miss that for anything."

"Who lives next door to you?"

"What? Over there?" She tossed her head. "The Comptons. He's a salesman. I guess that's why I asked if you were one. Around here you're either a farmer or a salesman. He practically kills himself taking in a territory spread over three states. He sells good farm equipment, doesn't sell junk. But he hasn't gotten rich."

"Oh, no?"

"Though they say he does better than anybody else around here and has squirreled away plenty. As for her, she never worked a day in her life as far as I know, doesn't even garden."

"And their son?"

She narrowed her eyes. She had a careful face that was stamped with knowledge of the earth. "You're not a relative of theirs?"

"Oh, no. But the boy ..."

"Steven. Not a bad kid really. He helps me out whenever I need him. But he's not one for schoolwork and he hangs out with the wrong crowd. Punks. That's what my husband calls them. But they all own their own bikes and love those contraptions better than their own lives. Go figure ..."

"Steven Compton ..." The words slipped slowly out of Grey's mouth.

"Yes, that's him. As I say, he's a good kid ... Anything wrong?"

"No. Thanks. I'll be on my way."

From that moment on, Grey was obsessed—or was it possessed—by Steven Compton. The sole pleasure of his day was no longer pouring over his books but the anticipation of watching the boys riding by single file on their bikes. The only release of the pleasant tension consuming him was to spot Steven, usually bringing up the rear.

His afternoon visits to Kyle Efferham's ended so abruptly that the farmer thought he'd somehow offended Grey. But the truth was Grey couldn't concentrate on anything but the Compton boy. With a mixture of humility and adoration. The material world melted away before him, erased by a sprinkling of imperceptible acid, and only he and Compton were left.

By mid-May, when the first roses started to color, Grey strolled into town every day. He usually waited under the awning of the café patiently licking an ice cream cone Hazel sold him. He was careful to make it last until Steven Compton and his buddies pulled up

on their bikes and headed into the café to stoke up on whatever
they stoked up on before they took the bikes on a run.

When the boys piled out of the café, they'd find him there,
under the awning, ice cream cone gone, his hands nonchalantly
in his trousers, but his face on fire and eyes avoiding Steven.

One of the boys nudged Steven and Grey heard him ask,
"Who's that guy hanging out here every day?"

"I don't know. He has the right to hang out wherever he wants.
Doesn't bother me."

One of the boys wasn't so sure. "Fucking weirdo," he yelled at
Grey and spit in his direction. "Freak." Grey stared down at his
shoes.

But even if he wanted, Steven couldn't ignore Grey's
attentions. Every morning, Steven woke up to find small
bouquets lying under his window, violets, peonies, miniature
roses chilled with dew. Though he never saw Grey put them
there, he knew it was him.

One morning he noticed a white card attached to some roses.
He went out to get it as his mom called him to breakfast. He
surreptitiously read the handwritten message: *You are a god,
perfect and enduring.*

At school, Steven sat at his desk all morning unable to stop
thinking about that mysterious note he'd brought with him to
look at from time to time. Until this morning, he'd never thought
much about his looks, even though he worked out. But now,
glancing around the class, he realized his features were superior
to the others. He had a handsome face, was powerfully built, and
made a commanding figure on his bike … Yes, that note told the
truth.

He showed his Ninja 400 off to some of the younger boys after
school. He let them clean and polish it until he could see his own
reflection in the metal.

Whenever he saw Grey hanging around the grocery, café, or park, he'd never look in his direction, but find some excuse to flex his pecs, broaden his chest, break into a wide, careless grin before mounting his Ninja, slowly, evenly, making every movement and gesture count. Instead of finding Grey disgusting or a creep, he realized he was necessary, the same way an audience is to an actor. He knew he could count on Grey to follow him back home at a discrete distance and wait across the road in the abandoned barn like a faithful bitch hoping for a glimpse of his master through the upstairs bedroom window.

Steven's buddies were surprised when he refused to join them for their afternoon cross-country rides. His excuse was that his old man was forcing him to stay at home until his grades improved.

When he was alone, he bent down by the porch, pretended to inspect his bike's tires, all the while watching from the corner of his eye for Grey to appear from around the bend. As soon as Grey came into view, staggering nervously as he slipped into the barn, Steven chained up the Ninja like a beast, headed inside, bounded up the stairs, opened his bedroom window and started exercising in front of it, doing some squats and overhead presses from his weight bench, adjusting the height of the barbell more often than he needed. When he'd had enough, Steven shut the window and pulled the shade.

Steven asked his dad to buy him a full-length mirror, explaining he wanted it to keep track of his muscle conditioning and development. Dad complied and one day they unloaded it from the rear of the truck and hammered it onto the back of the closet door in his bedroom. After that, Steven found it impossible to tear himself away from it.

One evening at sundown when the sky was heavy with red streaks, Steven discovered Grey crouched in the bushes below his window. No more hiding in the barn. Steven, his heart racing so loud he thought the world could hear it, slowly pulled off his shirt. He knew Grey could see him in the mirror through the window. Steven posed in front of it, showed off his muscles, did his squats and lifts and worked himself into a sweat.

The red in the sky was now covered with a slate of opaque blue though the red could still be seen burning underneath. But the room turned dark. Steven switched on the light in front of his window. He stared out towards the inky fields, eyes focused on nothing, and stroked his rigid stomach and ran his hands all over his abs and up to his nipples. Then his hands moved down to his shorts which he slowly lowered. Then he fingered his jockstrap.

From below he heard a soft moan, "No. No. No."

Furiously, Steven banged the window shut, latched it, and jerked the shade down.

Tim Grey was violently and mysteriously ill for one week. He ran a high fever. His mouth was bone dry and when he sipped at water, it only tasted like sand. When he recovered, he had no idea what had happened, what his ailment had been, why he'd fallen prey to whatever it was he had. After his fever subsided and he was falling asleep, he remembered coming home from town distraught, tearing through the fields at a monstrous pace, stumbling, bruising himself, practically crawling inside the house on all fours. Ridiculous. He'd been an animal running from the wind.

Grey paid more frequent visits to Kyle Efferham. The weather was unusually warm yet the breeze that crossed Efferham's porch was cool and tender. "Summer's wanting to come on in," Kyle claimed, "but spring won't let go yet." Once again, he started talking about his past, his teaching years, his wife, their contentment, while Kyle filled his ears with rumors about everybody in town until they broke apart in guffaws. Grey was lightening up, throwing something off his back.

When Efferham told some obscure story about the Comptons, it didn't affect Grey. He hardly thought about the boy now, in fact he never bothered looking out the window when the boys rode by in their ritualistic, afternoon processions. No, he was busy canning preserves. There were already raised beds of strawberries behind his farmhouse, a crop had ripened early. There were a lot of steps to canning ... preparing the berries, cooking them, sterilizing the jars, then ladling the hot preserves in the jars before submerging them in boiling water, and then the cooling process. It all took time, it kept him busy. But one evening Grey said something that Kyle Efferham found peculiar. He pointed into the twilight and muttered, "There's a white star coming for me." But it was a cloudy sky, starless, dull.

WHEN SPRING BURST INTO summer, Grey didn't notice. He was still absorbed by his strawberries. He took his canned preserves around to give as gifts to Kyle, the postman, to Hazel in the café. He almost took one to the next-door neighbor of the Comptons but decided against it.

He still paid no attention to the bikes that sped by his window every day. But one day, after the sounds of the bikes had disappeared, he looked out the window as a matter of course and was shocked to see Steven straddling his bike across the road and staring in at him. He seemed annoyed, almost pouting, waiting for something. Before Grey could react, Steven stared straight ahead and, right hand gripping the throttle, revved the engine, and shot off in a burst of raw energy.

That night there were showers, they weren't too heavy but the sound of the rain on the roof gave Grey an irregular sleep. He kept waking up, knowing he'd been dreaming about his past, in fact had gone deep into his past, but there was nothing concrete he could remember or take stock of, no images, no nightmares, no pleasant memories, nothing.

The next morning was unsurpassed for beauty. The June day was cold, cunning, yet sun crowded in everywhere and the scent of flowers swelled the breeze. Grey, finally rested, longed to be outdoors and he grabbed a pail and headed out back to pick strawberries. But then he thought of the Scots pines across the road from his farmhouse. He had a sudden desire to be among them. He dropped his pail, crossed the road and zigzagged through the trees, spotting new flowers that had shot up around them, protected by the shade and yet reached by the sun. It was so still that his footsteps seemed to echo.

He came into a small clearing surrounded by the pines whose orange bark glimmered like gold. He turned his head in surprise. There in the grove was Compton's black bike and stretched on top of it was Steven himself, naked, asleep. His head rested on the handlebars, his hair falling and trapping the sunbeams. His ass lay firm on the seat while his spread legs dangled by the wheels.

At first Grey was shocked, followed by the sudden return of the passionate suffering he'd felt so deeply.

Steven Compton stirred. He opened his eyes and turned his head toward Grey. Then he stretched and yawned. Grey was reminded of the drawings in his mythological books of beautiful young shepherds or gods resting in a sylvan glade.

Steven eased his muscular body off the bike and walked a few feet to a small pool that glistened. The water looked cold and clear. Steven knelt and bent over the pool and scooped a handful of water to drink, then wet his fingers and stroked his face of classic beauty.

So, Grey thought, that was it. The boy wouldn't let him alone. How had Steven come to be languidly stretched out, naked, on his bike across the road from where he lived? He was a seducer. An enticer. Yet he acted as if no one else was there but himself ...

Grey moved close to Steven, casually, but his brain was bursting. Sunlight filtered through the canopy of trees and made the crystal pool almost transparent. It was as if the boy was hovering over a feast of diamonds, so strong was the sun's reflection in the water. Grey crouched next to Steven, but the boy still didn't acknowledge him.

Tim Grey was transfixed by Steven's ivory chest where blond hairs stirred above his nipples. He swore he could see the boy's taut flesh moving in unison with the pumping of his heart. He desperately wanted to feel that chest, to lay his hand softly on Steven's warm skin.

He reached out but like a whip Steven slapped his hand away, then shoved Grey's head into the pool. Though Grey pushed back and fought with all his might, the boy was too strong, too sturdy, too capable. Grey's mouth burst open, and he was fed the diamonds. Steven held his head under the water with one hand and with the other brushed back his blond hair. He never took his eyes from his own reflection which sent him back his own beauty, from earth to water to air.

It wasn't long before Grey's body was discovered. His death was declared an unfortunate accident. He had paused for a drink of water and drowned. His niece from Ohio inherited Grey's farmhouse but she didn't want it and put it up for sale. A farmer who owned the land next to it bought it and razed it, converting it to a pasture for his cattle.

The years passed away and hardly anyone even remembered Tim Grey. Except for the inveterate gossip Kyle Efferham. After six or seven years, his tongue got loose one night as he sat drinking with a farmer from a neighboring county and he admitted he'd gone to look for Grey who hadn't shown up at his house for one of their usual talks. He'd seen young Steven Compton tearing away from the grove of pines on his bike, looking fierce as the devil himself.

Compton had aroused his suspicions, so he walked into the woods and discovered the body. Kyle couldn't figure out what Grey was doing down on his stomach, his face in a pool of water.

It was odd, to say the least. But it would have been unwise to tell his story to the sheriff and implicate Steven Compton. The boy had his whole life to look forward to, and after all, Kyle might have been wrong about the whole affair.

"Why, Steven Compton has a farm out by me," Kyle's farmer friend declared. "His dad gave him the money to start it up, wanted him to settle down. And he did. I can't figure Compton getting involved in something like that. The boy had no need for money. Wouldn't have no reason to go robbing anybody."

"No, I guess not," Efferham admitted.

He remembered stopping at the Compton farm a few months back to see if Steven would back a friend of his for county supervisor in the upcoming elections. Steven and his wife were doing just fine, though Steven himself had turned to fat and was exhausted by farm life and old before his time. But he had a bunch of kids running wild and they were good looking, they all took after him, sons and daughters with the lightest long hair and the most powerful brown eyes and the milkiest skin as if they'd spent their lives beneath umbrellas, yet they were never still a minute, were prodded on by some free spirit, disobeying their parents and poking their noses into everything forbidden.

WE'RE GOING PLACES

"LOOK WHO'S COMING DOWN the street," Adam Marsh called over to his lover, Bill Cooly, who was busy at the kitchen counter cutting up red and yellow peppers and some shallots to throw into a spring salad for dinner. "The professor."

"Oh, our landlord, you mean?" Bill turned to see Adam practically hanging out the window staring down at Max Brewster as he made his way toward the entrance to his brownstone situated "within spitting distance of the High Line" as Adam liked to say, just around the corner from 10th Avenue on the south side of 18th Street in Chelsea, currently Manhattan's trendiest neighborhood.

"Yes. Our rich landlord," Adam mused as he left his spot at the window to sit down at the sturdy wooden table in the middle of the kitchen. He picked up his cup of cinnamon tea and inhaled the aroma while studying his lover as he sliced the peppers.

Bill was pretty much of a control freak who had his vegetables lined up like ducks in a row, just waiting their turns to be chopped up. A squash, three carrots, two cucumbers, an eggplant. Eggplant, Adam wondered, was that a vegetable? And if so, did it spring up from the ground or did it grow on trees like coconuts? He would never have dreamed of asking Bill for the answer but would look it up online later. It wouldn't do to have the man he was going to marry find out that he didn't know what an eggplant was.

Adam turned his thoughts back to their landlord. "Max. He's surprisingly young to own this prime piece of real estate in New York City, don't you think? And much too green to be some kind of tycoon. How do you think he was able to get his hands on this building?"

"Inherited wealth," Bill answered. "He doesn't strike me as the type of young guy to be able to buy a brownstone like this all on his own. He's too laid back."

"He's not like you, is he?" Adam asked pointedly. "Having been able to rely on a fabulous salary all these years."

Bill winced slightly, not at the fabulous salary part, but at the all these years part. "We'll be in the position to buy a chic apartment in Chelsea ourselves," Adam announced. "Renting from Max is only temporary. A port in a storm while we look around for our own place."

"Hmm," Bill mumbled. Then almost absentmindedly added, "It's a nice port in a storm, though."

"Of course it is, darling," Adam said. "That's not what I meant. Anyway, back to Max. We've never seen his mom pull up in a limo fresh from a 5th Avenue shopping spree, have we? Or a dapper dad strolling down the block, his arm around Max's shoulder, whispering some financial advice in his ear. Do you think they're both dead, then? His parents? That's what you mean by inherited wealth?"

"That was just an educated guess. You're too curious for your own good, Adam. Remember—"

"Spare me," Adam interrupted him, getting up from the kitchen table and strolling into the living room where he threw himself down onto their white leather sofa. "I know," he called back into the kitchen. "Curiosity killed the cat."

Bill nodded to himself as he finished slicing the second to the last of the red peppers then moved to the kitchen doorway where he stood, hands on his hips, staring at Adam who was casually flipping through a glitzy magazine on interior design. Adam tossed the magazine onto a low glass coffee table and looked up at Bill before asking, "But then, what's life without curiosity?"

"Pleasant and pain free," Bill assured him.

At least it was for Bill. For over twenty years he'd been one of the stars of a major daytime soap opera and though he was forty-five, he had aged well and was still considered tall, dark and handsome, according to his fans at least. He got plenty of exercise, had a fat checkbook and no financial worries, and he made a few visits to the plastic surgeon's for a subtle nip and tuck when nobody was looking. Oh, yes, and he had Adam, sweet, blond, and twenty- four, a cherry blossom that would stay pink for years. Bill felt he was just entering the prime of his life, surrounded by all the trimmings any sane man could desire.

"It's not just Max I'm curious about," Adam said thoughtfully, "but about everybody who lives in this building."

Bill joined him on the sofa and playfully slapped him in the stomach with one of the end pillows. "What are you going on about? We're just a group of tenants like any others you'd find living along the High Line."

"Only a little more unconventional."

Bill couldn't see it. But they had only been here three months, not much time to carefully observe the other tenants who lived in this cozy brownstone, only six stories high.

"I'm mainly talking about our straight arrow landlord Max, living alone in his ground-floor apartment," Adam said. "We're on the second in a floor-through—"

"I'm well aware of the layout," Bill interrupted.

"Well, there's that sexy Celina who Max installed in the studio on the top floor. That singer from Cajun country in Louisiana. She's obviously his mistress. Though they seem exact opposites."

"Nothing wrong with that."

Adam shrugged. "No, I'm interested in figuring people out, that's all."

Bill was on to him. "You mean how they climbed the ladder to success? Isn't that it?" Adam shrugged.

"Some people are quite clever," Bill said. "There's your answer. And Celina might simply be Max's girlfriend, not mistress."

Adam sniffed. "All right. Girlfriend. We'll have it your way."

Bill wondered if Adam had too much time on his hands. Sometimes he acted as if he were to the manor born, only he wasn't. Of course neither was Bill who'd only become rich because of his long-lasting part on a TV soap opera. He wanted to protect that goldmine.

When Bill signed the lease with Max, he'd had his lawyer insert a clause in it that forbade Max from disclosing to anyone that Bill was gay and lived with another man. It would be ruinous for his female fans to find out the truth. As for Adam, he'd been crammed into a Hell's Kitchen studio only a few months ago with two other guys and had barely been able to make ends meet when he and Bill had met at a Mexican restaurant near Bill's studio. A few margaritas later and the rest was history. Bill sold his house in the suburbs, gave up his onerous commute, rented this apartment and moved an unemployed Adam, twenty odd years his junior, in with him, lock stock and barrel, put his name on the lease and vouched for him financially.

Bill had the distinct impression that while Max had respect for him, he didn't think much of his lover Adam, or the fact he'd lifted Adam, when he'd least expected it, out of his Hell's Kitchen hole and into the stratosphere. Although Max wasn't much older than Adam, he came off as a serious guy and Bill sensed, as Max went about renovating and leasing apartments in a brownstone he owned, that he disapproved of Adam whiling away his hours by hanging out windows.

Or dining indolently with Bill on their little balcony that overlooked the garden.

The balcony was a feature that was unique to their apartment. Since they weren't high enough up to have a view of the High Line from their living room, which looked directly underneath it at its cement belly, Max had built a little balcony off their kitchen, on the opposite side of the High Line, just above the garden, as a kind of recompense. The addition of the balcony made that particular apartment more desirable when it came to renting it out. It was a nice feature for Max to be able to offer.

Now that the evenings were warm, Adam and Bill would sit on their balcony well into the night, hours after they'd finished up their dinner, watching and listening to the other tenants if they happened to be in the garden, otherwise just enjoying the greenery and each other's company.

That evening when Max walked into the garden, he saw that Adam and Bill happened to be dining up on their favorite perch.

"Max," Adam called out. "Come join us for a glass of wine or a spot of coffee."

"Oh, not tonight, I'm pretty busy. But thanks for the offer."

"Another time, then?" Adam asked.

"Yes, absolutely," Max replied, giving the garden a once-over to be sure everything was in order.

"Well, Max, we're good for a rain check at the hour of your choosing," Adam informed him. "We want to get to know you better."

"Sure thing," Max said. It was easy for Adam to say they wanted to get to know him better. Max, however, per the decree in their lease, was forbidden to even acknowledge their relationship. But he realized that underneath everything, Adam and Bill were friendly enough and that he was fortunate to have them as his tenants. Their idle banter wasn't that different from any other couple's, he supposed. "OK, guys, good night," he called up to them.

"Good night," they called back, preoccupied. Adam was trying to string a garland of ivy along the balcony railing.

Bill warned Adam, "Be sure you wash your hands after handling that. It could be poison ivy and an actor can't afford a scarred face."

"I know poison ivy when I see it," Adam groaned. "And this is not it."

A breeze came in off the Hudson and rustled through the ivy and the pink and white peonies in the flower bed, and the new leaves on the maple Max had planted in the center of the garden. An ivory moon lent its glow to the garden and to a contented Bill and Adam.

After dinner, Adam did the dishes while Bill sat at the kitchen table finishing a glass of red wine while going over his lines in tomorrow's script.

"Bill, wouldn't it be fun to have our wedding right on the High Line?" Adam asked.

Bill looked up. "Adam," he said with a serious edge. "We have to be discreet about all of this you know. I'm not out. Our wedding has to be kept a secret."

"I was joking." Adam wiped a plate dry and kept his back to Bill. "Still, there's an irony here somewhere. We're going to be married legally in the state of New York yet we have to keep it quiet. But I can dream about being able to send out announcements to our friends and family, get our names on a register for wedding gifts, even have a publicized honeymoon. Like that skater Johnny Weir who took his husband Viktor to the Dominican Republic."

Bill choked on his wine and spit out a mouthful that ended up all over the pages of his script, turning them a bright red. Adam calmly assessed the situation, bringing Bill a glass of water and some paper towels. While Bill wiped up the spill and tried to figure out if he could still decipher his lines, Adam continued, "They bought a house in New Jersey, you know, and I read that Johnny can't wait to get Viktor interested in his fabulous collection of Fabergé eggs."

It was impossible. Bill couldn't make out a word on the page. "Adam," he said, "didn't I read that they got a divorce quite some time ago?"

"Oh, really?" Adam was shocked, his picture of marital bliss slightly darkened.

Bill continued, "Anyway, I suspect I have a little different fan base than Johnny Weir."

Later they gathered around the computer in the small study. Adam said, "Before dinner I was trying to see if I could find out some information online about our neighbors but your name is the only one of the whole lot that comes up. Bill Cooly. There are entries about you from Honolulu to Stockholm."

"And I'd like to keep it that way. It shows my fans are thinking about me."

Adam googled Max for the second time but was thwarted. "Funny, Max doesn't have any entries. As the owner of this building, you'd think his name would pop up somewhere. But not under Max Brewster, not even Maximilian Brewster."

"You have to have done something noteworthy or illegal to 'pop up.' You'll find his name by looking up his building in the city registry."

"I found your age too," Adam said, brushing a few locks of his blond hair back from his forehead. "I was horrified."

"Age is just a number."

"Absolutely. And you wear your number well. Still, most people would like to be able to keep that number to themselves."

"Adam, let me get this straight. You wouldn't mind our wedding announcement being trumpeted all over the internet, pictures of the ceremony on social media, but you'd like to keep my age hidden? The ability to dole out selective information doesn't exist anymore."

Frustrated that there hadn't been any information to glean about any of their fellow tenants online, Adam realized he was going to have to rely on his intuition to figure them all out.

At least during his pre-dinner research he'd found out that eggplants come from the nightshade family, the same family as the potato, tomato, and sweet pepper, and that, heavy as they are, they grow on vines (!), and have a pleasantly bitter taste and spongy texture, like certain male appendages. However, in the end, it was still unclear whether an eggplant was a fruit or a vegetable.

Bill stood up and stretched. "I'm bushed. I'm off to bed."

"I'd like to taste your nightshade tonight," Adam purred.

"What?"

"Your eggplant."

"Oh, no. On a normal night, fine, but I have to get to the studio early to find a clean script and go over the lines I can't read now, the ones you caused me to spill wine on."

"I'm not tired at all," Adam complained, shooting him a sexy look.

"Not tonight, Adam. It's lights out and no funny business." Bill stumbled toward the bedroom. "And by the way, you had no luck in persuading me our neighbors are worthy of any further interest or investigation."

As Bill disappeared into the bedroom, Adam silently disagreed. Their neighbors hadn't put their cards on the table yet, that's all. Most people held their cards tight to their chests, if the truth be told, and only when it really mattered would they reveal their hands.

ADAM SAT ON THE sidelines of a sound stage at the New Century Studio on West 55th Street and 12th Avenue watching Bill rehearse a scene for his soap *To Love, Honor and Disobey*. Adam had pestered Bill for months to allow him to come to a shoot, and Bill had finally agreed on the grounds that if anybody asked him who he was, Adam would pretend to be his cousin from Virginia.

Bill played Dr. Timothy Grange, a revered GP whose father, one of those TV evergreens, a Wall Street investor who had made billions—it had never been revealed just how—had installed Timothy and his family in a mansion on the beach in East Hampton. Bill's co-star in the scene was a tall, glacial actress named Tandy Marlowe. She played his wife, Francine.

From what Adam had deduced from watching the show for the last month or so in the comfort of their own living room, Francine was an auburn-haired gold digger beneath her carefully cultivated, wifely persona.

The scene they were rehearsing took place in Dr. Timothy Grange's study. The director, a brash redhead named Miranda Schule, had made Bill and Tandy rehearse the brief scene over and over, yet Miranda asked them to run through it once more.

Adam wondered who she'd slept with to get her job. He debated whether it was sexist to assume she had, but decided it wasn't, since Bill had informed him that everybody connected with the show, male and female, had ended up either sleeping with each other or some higher up they hoped would further their careers. The #MeToo movement hadn't changed much around here.

"You mean they'd hop into bed with just anybody?" Adam had asked.

"Except the stage door cat."

That begged the question, who was it Bill had slept with? But Adam didn't pry further. Whoever he'd slept with, it was over now and there was nothing Adam could do about it. He and Bill both had to start from scratch in that department.

Bill and Tandy—rather Dr. Grange and his wife, Francine—started rehearsing the scene again.

Francine rushed into her husband's study without knocking, surprising Dr. Grange as he sat at his desk, passively shuffling through some notes.

He looked up. "Is something the matter?" His wife shot him a withering look.

He sought safer ground. "Did you enjoy your walk along the beach?"

"Not particularly. I couldn't stop thinking about the bomb you dropped at Chip Evans' party last night."

Dr. Timothy Grange regarded her curiously.

"Also, if you must know," Francine added petulantly, "the beach was cold and it started to rain, hardly ideal for a walk."

"May I ask just what bomb you're referring to?"

"The fact that you didn't deny you had a college affair with Glen Petty when that snob, that self-proclaimed arbiter of East Hampton society, Lorna Glennings, asked you whether or not it was true. You just stood there with an insipid smile on your face while I nearly died from embarrassment."

"That's not what I would call a bomb but a cheap shot that didn't deserve an answer."

"Did you know," Francine asked, slamming her fist on his desk, "that right after that, Mark Reynolds, our town alderman, brought me over a drink and asked if it was true that my husband was gay? He'd obviously overheard."

"I hope you advised him it was a baseless rumor."

"In my own way. I told him, 'Hell, no, he's not gay. And I should know!'"

"That settles it."

"No. Once the whispers start, it's too late. Don't you realize how a rumor like that could destroy your practice? You'll wake up one morning and wonder why the patients you've cultivated all these years have suddenly become 'no-shows' ... only to find out they've been going to a different doctor. A straight one!"

"Francine, for God's sake, you know I'm not gay. I never had an affair with Glen Petty," he insisted.

"Then why didn't you deny it? As far as I'm concerned your reputation has taken a big hit."

"Darling," Dr. Grange got up from his desk, came around to his wife and took her by the shoulders. Looking deeply into her eyes, he insisted, "My reputation is beyond reproach."

She broke away from him, annoyed. "There's a scandal brewing, and I won't stay and be a part of it. I didn't spend years turning this mansion into a showplace, making sure our children attended the most exclusive schools, seeing that our family was accepted in East Hampton society, all to have it disappear in a puff of smoke because it comes out you've been leading a closeted life as a homosexual."

Grange chafed at that. "So now you're calling me a homosexual. Next you'll be saying I cruise the East Hampton beaches looking for pick-ups. My patients would never believe that. And I don't give a damn about what anybody else thinks. My patients are the ones I care about. They have my heart."

"Well, somebody should have your back." Francine paused. "You're a selfish man, Timothy Grange ... You may end up giving them your heart. But not your money. And not this East Hampton mansion." She whirled out of the room with a sweeping gesture of finality.

But Tandy, *aka* Francine, stayed on the set, deep in thought, and it wasn't long before she called the director and Bill over for a little *tête-à-tête*.

"Miranda," Tandy complained to the director, "this is just not working."

"Why not?" Miranda Schule asked.

"Francine would be more subtle about bringing this delicate subject up to her husband. She wouldn't hit him over the head with it from the get-go."

"Uh-uh," Miranda disagreed. "She's The Bitch. That's how the viewers know you and that's how they want you. They aren't going to buy strawberries and cream dripping from your lips. The only important thing you have to keep in mind is that you're a complete and utter bitch."

"You mean that Francine is a complete and utter bitch."

"I was referring to your character."

"*My* character?"

"Francine's character. I wasn't talking about your personal attributes." Miranda smiled sweetly.

"All right, then." Tandy crossed her arms and capitulated. "I'm The Bitch, my audience wants The Bitch, and they've got The Bitch."

Miranda sighed. "Glad you put that one together."

"Not so fast," Tandy said. "One more thing. This is a stinking script."

Adam could see Bill standing like a bowling pin between the two women, secretly sweating bullets, but remaining upright for now. But if somebody bowled a strike ... Adam remembered Bill saying once, "I don't give a flying fuck about my character or the scripts, just my paycheck. This thing ain't art but it sure is a science."

Miranda, after taking a measured beat, asked, "How so?"

Tandy explained. "It's confusing when I say to my husband that he may give his heart to his patients but he's not about to give them his money or East Hampton mansion. The erstwhile Dr. Grange wouldn't give his money or his mansion to his patients … not the Dr. Grange I've worked with over twenty years … Aren't I right, Bill?"

Bill was too busy wilting under the lights to respond. He dug at his shirt collar. Adam felt kind of sorry for him and he usually didn't feel sorry for other people all that much.

"Don't drag Bill into this, this is your fight, Tandy."

"Miranda, this is not a fight."

"It has the ring of one to me."

"Tandy, how do you see the dialogue changing?" Bill offered discreetly.

"I'll show you. Hit me with those last lines again."

Bill fed her the line about giving his heart to his patients.

Francine let loose. "You're a selfish man, Timothy Grange. But I half realized that when I married you. You may end up giving them your heart. To your patients, that is. But if you do, your family may end up losing what you've worked so hard to give us. Financial stability. Which is tied to the worth of this East Hampton mansion, which is what we stand to lose, darling, if it ever came out that you really did sleep with Glen Petty. Don't you see?"

And Bill had actually figured Tandy would improve the thing.

"Damn," Miranda said. "You just put me to sleep in seven sentences. You've destroyed this woman's fire, her angst. Think Medea, fighting tooth and nail to save herself and her children from her wrongheaded do-gooder of a husband with a newly discovered kinky side. The lines are perfect as they are."

A tempest in a teapot, Adam thought. But this was show business, as unpredictable, exhilarating, and combustible as a good boxing match. He'd had enough of it however and left the building to take a break outside. He sat on a stone wall opposite the stage door exit and stared at the sun poking between two skyscrapers. It was about as exciting as watching an ant race. But more exciting than seeing Francine Grange flip out one more time at what she considered her husband's wilfulness. He was surprised when Bill came out shortly afterwards and ushered him into a cab to go back to their apartment.

"Whose side did you come down on?" Bill asked after informing Adam they were postponing shooting the scene until tomorrow.

"Yours. Let the two women fight to the death over a few words here and there. You were right to keep your nose clean. The key is to never take anybody's side about anything. Always play dumb and stay neutral."

"I plan to." He frowned. "But I have to say I don't particularly like this new direction the storyline is going in. The hint that I could have a gay side. That's sure to upset my fans."

"Don't be silly. Have you been hiding under a rock or something? Viewers want—no, demand—gay characters these days. Or queer characters I should say. Well, one should actually say LGBTQQUO2SAA characters."

"I don't even want to know."

Adam pulled a card out of his wallet. "I'm trying to memorize them. Let's see, they're acronyms for Lesbian, Gay, Bisexual, Transgender, Queer, Questioning, Intersex, Pansexual, Two-Spirit, Androgynous, and finally Asexual."

"Well, that last one isn't you. And please never read that list to me again. That's a once-in-a-lifetime thrill."

Adam put his little cheat sheet back in his wallet. "Well, you have to keep up. I think the ball started rolling when two young gay guys kissed on *Days of Our Lives* years ago. Now they can't put that horse back in the barn."

"That's all well and good, but soap fans who've followed a character for years suddenly don't want that character to change into somebody else. My fans all know me as Dr. Grange, a happily married man. At least they did until today."

"Then you'd better ask the writers to stress that you're still having plenty of sex with your wife. Play a few scenes with your shirt off."

"That's for the younger guys on the show." As he said it a chill ran down his spine. He was no heartthrob anymore, no testosterone-filled romantic lead. In fact he was a breath away from character parts. Or, apparently, if the story editors decided, a breath away from playing older gay men. His lips went dry.

"I suppose you're right," Adam said. "There are plenty of young bucks on their way up. Life passes us by so fast."

His words made Bill feel worse. But he hid his discomfort with a burst of frivolity. "So says the young whippersnapper."

Adam laughed gaily. "Do you like my haircut?" he asked. "I got it specifically in time for the rehearsal."

From what Bill could tell, it was just a standard trim. "It's nice," he commented.

"I wanted to look my best, just in case people put two and two together and figured you and I—"

"Adam."

"Those things have a way of coming out into the open when you least expect it."

Bill spat out between gritted teeth, "Those things won't come out if you keep your goddamn mouth shut."

"It's not me you should be worried about. You said the crew at the door might ask what my connection to you was, but they didn't." Annoyed at having been cursed at, he took a dig at Bill. "Maybe because they already guessed what that connection was."

Bill was incensed. "If they did, then that's the end of your meal ticket. Because I won't have a job anymore."

Adam crossed his arms. "I don't like the man I'm going to marry advising me that he's my meal ticket."

"It was a poor choice of words. I'm sorry."

The cab pulled up in front of their apartment building and the driver eyed them both with interest as Bill settled the fare. For the second time that afternoon a chill went down Bill's spine. Could it be the cab driver had heard everything and knew who he was?

As Bill let them into their second floor apartment, he realized there were cab drivers, and Uber and Lyft drivers, paid by gossip columnists to hang around studio doors and purposely pick up celebrities, listen to their unguarded conversations then report back to these vultures who slipped them cash for a piece of their privacy. If the gossip writers got something salacious, they'd publish it, confident it would lead to some celebrity's downfall and pave the way for additional stories about the following rack and ruin.

BILL WATCHED AS ADAM sauntered in from the bathroom after washing up and threw himself down on the couch, piling a couple of pillows behind his head. "I'm tuckered out!" he exclaimed as if he'd been the one who'd just gone through the rigors of rehearsing that day.

For a moment Bill wondered, really wondered, if Adam was the type to secretly sell their story to some gossip monger, not for profit, but to get his own spot in the limelight. He thought hard but in the end decided no. Adam was just a good kid who was excited to be marrying a soap opera star. If his exuberance sometimes overshot its defined boundaries, like the fizz from a Coke spilling onto a glass table top, no harm was meant and no harm done.

Later, after sharing a brief dinner on their balcony, Bill, who seemed antsy, disappeared into the kitchen and returned with a copy of "it," the script Adam thought he'd seen the last of when he'd walked out of the studio door that afternoon. "I think I need to rewrite some of Francine's lines for tomorrow," he said. "I'm not supposed to, of course, it's against Guild rules, but I'm going to anyway, to show the powers that be there's a better direction to take this thing in."

Bill opened the script to that controversial section of dialogue. "Let's see. Francine is going to have to stand up more for her husband, not play into the negative comments made at the party about him, stress his masculinity."

"But you *are* masculine."

"You know it, I know it, and everybody on the show knows it. But when the writers suddenly say the sky is red, you have to convince them they've made a mistake, remind them that the sky is as blue as it's always been. You see what I mean?"

"Vaguely."

"Vaguely? TV is a writer's medium and the wordsmiths who put this little scene together are highly paid. But they fucked up. Is that any less vague?"

Adam said, "I hate to see you stressed out like this."

"I've got a solution," Bill crowed. "How about Francine taking her husband's side at Chip Evans' party when that arbiter of East Hampton society, Lorna Glennings, insinuates Dr. Grange had an affair with Glen Petty. Francine tells her husband, 'Don't worry, dear, she's making it all up, getting revenge because she thinks you didn't do enough to save her husband from dying of pneumonia.' And then when Mark Reynolds, the town alderman, brings them a drink and confronts them about the rumor, Francine says, 'My husband is a stud with real staying power. He's completely heterosexual. I ought to know. I won't have his virility questioned by a bitter old bitch and a full time drunk.'"

"Bill ..." Adam made a gesture of sticking his finger down his throat and throwing up.

"All right, all right, I made Francine overly defensive ... for some reason," Bill said, shaking his head. Then, "To hell with it." He threw the script on the floor.

Adam had just the antidote for making Bill feel better and to put everything out of his mind and it wasn't sex. He invited Max and his girlfriend to share a bottle of wine with them on their balcony. For once, Max was in the mood to accept the invitation. Max escorted Celina, chic, with white upswept hair, down from the top floor studio he'd renovated just for her. The four of them drank wine into the night on Bill's little balcony, Celina even singing a few jazz tunes *a capella* for them. It seemed she was getting some gigs around town already and becoming known in hip circles.

At one point, Adam's mind wandered back to the script. When he considered which version was best, the original writers, Tandy's, or Bill's, the writers' version won hands down. Though they all sucked. He'd like to have a crack at it himself, Bill had just said writers made a fortune conjuring up this kind of crap. Why shouldn't he try? Bill had quite a following. Celina was already getting gigs. And Max owned the damn building. Adam felt the odd man out.

BUT CIRCUMSTANCES SURROUNDING THE script were to change dramatically and only in a week. Bill and Tandy were summoned to a dinner by Miranda.

Miranda had chosen the open air restaurant on the rooftop of The Pearl, a boutique hotel overlooking the High Line, as well as the shops and restaurants in the Meatpacking District and the Hudson River beyond. They sat at one of the linen-covered tables arranged around the outdoor swimming pool under a canopy of faintly twinkling stars. Adam had insisted on joining them even if it meant he still had to pretend to be Bill's cousin from Virginia. Bill didn't protest. He sensed trouble brewing and was actually relieved by Adam's company.

Throughout dinner, the four of them sat there morosely, making occasional small talk, and picking at their food. Adam couldn't help noticing Julienne Hughes, a Hollywood star who was filming scenes for her new picture in the neighborhood, at the next table alongside her lover Roy. He'd seen their photos on the internet only last night. Julienne was wearing an expensive looking raspberry-tinged beaded cocktail dress while Roy was clad only in a pair of tight white swim trunks. They seemed lost in each other's company.

Adam turned back to his own party, with nothing much to consider except for Tandy's hair, swept up on her head like layers of burnished autumn leaves. His reverie was interrupted by Miranda who, finishing her dessert, said, "It's nice to finally meet you, Adam."

Adam shot a look at Bill. He shrugged.

"Likewise. Though it's like I know you already," Adam answered politely.

"Now you," she said to Tandy, tapping her fingers on the table for emphasis, "should have brought Cyril along."

"Are you out of your mind? He'd have been bored stiff!"

"He might perk up when he hears what you have to tell him when you get home."

"Out with it, Miranda," Tandy said. "It's obvious you think Cyril should be here to give me moral support. You've been dying to tell us something all night."

"To be frank, I've been dying *not* to tell you while I've been choking my way through my meal." She paused. "I'm afraid I have some unpleasant news for you and Bill. The soap's been cancelled."

"Why?" Tandy exclaimed.

"Soaps in general are tanking," Miranda said. "Correction. They *have* tanked. And ours is no exception."

Bill became defensive. "I thought ours was highly ranked."

"You fell asleep, Bill. That was some time ago. There are only two or three soaps left on the air. They're passé. They've been replaced by a freaking, glitzy meteor storm of sexy, glamorous extravaganzas full of gorgeous young stars with tits and abs stretching on *ad infinitum*. Middle age is out and hidden away on the high-numbered channels."

"So watching a good drama isn't enough anymore?" Bill asked, shaken.

"It seems what today's audience wants most are reality shows, to be able to experience the immediate thrill of being in a Roman arena with the ability to give a thumbs up or down to contestants desperate to make it. They want to see real blood spilt, somebody crowned champion."

"Whereas," Tandy said, "we're merely actors, not circus performers."

"Or Roman gladiators," Bill added glumly.

Adam tried to picture Bill in gladiator garb, complete with sword and sandals.

"It's unfortunate but viewers want to see real people suffer in a battle to stay on top, not imaginary characters doing the same thing," Miranda revealed.

Tandy continued sotto voce, "So, *To Love, Honor and Disobey* is now officially dead, that's what you're telling us, isn't it?"

"As of next week we're wrapping it up. Your contracts will be honored for the remainder of the season, of course."

"We'll still be getting checks on a regular basis from reruns." Bill was looking on the bright side, trying to take this upsetting news in stride.

"Bill," Miranda said, "this ain't forty years ago. No one wants to rerun soaps. They're dinosaurs."

"I've always wondered what it would be like to wake up one morning and find I'd turned into a brontosaurus," Tandy quipped.

"Look," Miranda leveled, "this whole thing fucks me over too. I just lost a lucrative directing gig. But I know the producers of *Survivor*. And I'm contacting them tomorrow, pronto."

"Is that show still on the air?" Bill asked.

"I hope to God it is," Miranda said. "When does *Survivor* come on?" she asked Julienne and Roy at the neighboring table.

"That thing where they throw you in the jungle with a bunch of over-energized pythons and tarantulas?" Julienne asked distastefully. "It's been off the air for years!"

"It's still on, honey," her sexy squeeze Roy said. "Or some offshoot of it. I just watched it."

Adam realized Miranda didn't recognize Julienne. He purposely didn't let on that Julienne was a big movie star or she'd have been over at their table trying to worm a gig out of her. Why should Miranda get any help? Shouldn't Bill get the first shot at Julienne? Or for that matter, why shouldn't Adam approach her for himself?

Bill asked with resignation, "So we tape our last segment next week?"

"Yes. And we've given you a juicy part. You actually admit to Francine not only that you did have that goddamned affair with Glen Petty but that you're as gay as Liberace."

Bill wiped the corner of his mouth with a napkin. "Charming."

"Oh, Bill, forget it," Adam said, looking out of the corner of his eye at Julienne, coveting her star status. "You're worth more than all these pygmies making these big decisions. You and me—we're going places."

Miranda said, "Well! So Spake Zarathustra."

Julienne had overheard most of their conversation and her interest was piqued. She gave the nod to Roy who dutifully moved behind her and pulled her chair back. Julienne stood up and addressed the four diners at the table next to hers. "You certainly have had a spirited discussion tonight. I loved it. But as for me, I don't believe in getting so wrought up over anything at this hour." She rubbed her hands over Roy's naked chest. "I believe in mellowing out after dinner. Heading upstairs to sex it up in a luxurious hotel suite. Now that keeps the blood pressure under the radar, doesn't it, Roy?"

Adam swore he saw Roy's bulge start to grow in his swim trunks. Bill saw it too.

"Hopefully, it keeps everything under the radar," Roy answered, grinning, rearranging himself as indiscreetly as possible. "But you can never be sure," he said, slipping his arm around Julienne's waist. "Peace." They walked off together, her head on his shoulder.

Bill and Adam hadn't been the only ones who'd noticed.

"Lover boy seemed to have a big snake hidden in full sight," Miranda mused with a mixture of longing and annoyance.

"How the hell is that going to help any of us?" Tandy snapped. "Our day will dawn tomorrow without him. And I imagine one day it will for her, too. As for me, I'm totally free now. We all are, so let's make the most of it." Tandy came up behind Bill, leaned over and kissed him on the cheek. "For the last twenty years you've been a wonderful husband to me, but now Timothy and Francine Grange can rest in peace."

SURPRISINGLY, IT WAS ADAM who decided to put off the wedding until after the honeymoon in Tahiti.

A December wedding was just the thing these days with the city all festive and brightly lit for Christmas. He told Bill that he'd read that in New York at least, December had surpassed June in popularity for tying the knot in all categories: bride and groom, bride and bride, groom and groom. That was because it was hard to find a vacant lawn and canopy in June now that gay marriage had come on the books. Bill accepted Adam's explanation at face value. He shouldn't have. Adam had made it all up, assuaging his guilt at lying to his lover by imagining that it was likely to be true.

To be honest, Bill didn't care what month they were getting married. He was happy to be lying in a hammock on the deck of their outer-water bungalow at Le Méridien's resort hotel in Bora Bora. Their flight by helicopter from Papeete to Bora Bora had lasted forty-five minutes, and they had been treated to some of the most spectacular scenery on the face of the earth, cloud-shrouded verdant islands, one after the other, sprouting up out of a light blue sea.

And on the shuttle to the hotel, the thought had come to Bill that he was somehow home, in the place he was meant to be.

"Tahiti is beyond my wildest dreams," he told Adam who was swinging a little restlessly in the hammock next to his.

"It's a culture shock," Adam said. "No dirty streets, no pushing and shoving crowds, and a quiet that's ringing in my ears. I have to get used to it. It's so remarkably beautiful here, it hardly seems real."

"Well, my boy, right now you're relaxing in a hammock on a lagoon off a spectacular coral reef. It's real. Pinch yourself."

"I'd rather not."

Adam was enchanted by his surroundings, he had to admit it. The individual bungalows were what he supposed would be referred to as "tastefully appointed" in traditional Polynesian decor, lots of white everywhere and brown twiny ropes and masks on the wall, those kinds of things. Each of the bungalows had an outdoor terrace that looked out onto an endless expanse of ocean. Some had views of Mount Otemanu, but theirs didn't. Adam would have liked that, some landmark to seize on and stare at, to remind him there was land around somewhere. But he could hardly complain. Their terrace had steps leading down into the water of the lagoon as if the whole of it belonged to them personally, and under their main living area were glass floor panels through which they could view sundry corals, plants, and fishes of various sizes, shapes, and colors, all day long.

"No one to disturb us here," Bill chuckled. "No call for makeup or a last minute change in my lines. That's all in the past."

A huge white bird spread its wingspan in the air above them and hovered effortlessly as the breeze seemed to have no power to move it along.

"Look up above you, that's an albatross if I'm not mistaken," Bill said to Adam.

A middle-aged man with a British accent who was energetically passing along the walkway, presumably heading to his own bungalow, said, "No, no. That's a giant frigatebird. Couldn't help but overhear. Voices do carry out over the water. Hope you don't mind my correcting you."

"You mean informing us," Bill corrected him. "No, not at all."

He was going to introduce himself but the man had disappeared. Well, he'd do it later. Out here there was plenty of time.

"I wish that bird would go on," Adam shouted. "It's gigantic and weird. It's like it's staring down at us."

"Keep your voice a little lower," Bill warned. "That Brit's right. Voices carry out here, and it wouldn't do to let him hear that you're afraid of some bird."

Voices carried, Adam thought, and what else? The sounds of him and Bill making love later? Would the other bungalow dwellers be able to hear that? What a laugh. In the heart of New York City, with thousands of people crammed in boxes next to you, no one would be able to hear you scream with passion. But here it seemed a handful of guests would be treated to your every soft moan and whimper.

Bill didn't have to wait long to introduce himself to the British gentleman because that same evening as he and Adam were enjoying the dinner buffet at Le Tipanie, a candle-lit semi-enclosed restaurant at their hotel, helping themselves to mouth-watering portions of fresh fruit at the buffet table, they happened to bump into their birdwatching neighbor and his wife.

"We meet again," Bill said. "I'm Bill and this is Adam."

"Oh, hello," the man said, "I'm Lewis Blackwater and this is my wife, Helen." Then he said in an aside to her, "They're our new neighbors. Bungalow eight."

"Oh," she said. "We're in nine."

Adam thought the couple oddly mismatched as Helen was tall, thin, and serious, and her husband, Lewis, rotund, red-faced, with laugh lines around his eyes and mouth. Helen said to Bill, graciously, "It's nice to meet you. Is Adam your son, I presume? There is a slight resemblance there."

A brief moment passed as history was being made. For the first time, Bill said simply, "No, I'm afraid not. We're lovers."

"Oh," Helen said, putting her hand to her neck, "forgive me. Of course, you're quite close in age after all. I see that now." She looked helplessly at her husband, whose jaw was slack and whose mouth hung open.

This time it was Adam who spoke up, "Oh, no, you were right. We're not close in age at all. Still, we're going to be married."

"Tell them what you do, dear," Helen said quickly to her husband.

"I'm a retired executive for British Airways," he said. Then after a moment he broke into laughter. "And I'm sure I don't look it either, first appearances being deceiving and whatnot. I look a right queer dickie-bird, I suppose, like Sherlock Holmes's

Watson. The film version." Then he shook hands heartily with both Adam and Bill. "Welcome to the South Pacific, gentlemen."

"Tell them what you do these days, dear, not what you did in the past," his wife chided him, her voice a little high-pitched and insistent.

"Oh, that's easy," Lewis said expansively. "I like to swim, fish, and snorkel. There's a lively fish and coral life to explore right here at the hotel. I recommend you take advantage."

"Oh, we will, thanks," Bill said. "I'm a retired soap opera star by the way."

"Is that right? Now that's something different," Lewis said.

"How exciting," his wife added with a gleam in her eyes.

Later, back at their table, as Adam was looking proudly at Bill for the first time, he was reminded that voices did carry out here over the lagoon. From the Blackwaters' table some distance away, they heard Helen say to her husband, "Well, each new rich day, I must say. Wait till they hear about this back home. I'm sure this type of thing goes on all the time in London, not so much in Milton Keynes."

"I was speechless," Lewis Blackwater replied. "You were giving me the push to keep up the conversation and I had no idea what to say to those gay blokes."

"You did just fine. In a situation like that, there is no right or wrong. But I was proud of how you handled it."

Adam took Bill's hand and held it under the table and looked into his lover's eyes and purposely repeated Helen's words to him, "You did just fine. In a situation like that there is no right or wrong. But I was proud of how you handled it."

That night they made love loudly and vociferously and if any bungalow dwellers happened to hear them, Adam thought, they could just eat their hearts out.

THE NEXT DAY, BILL brought Adam by helicopter to Rangiroa, one of the outer islands of the Tahitian chain. The helicopter guide had been born and raised there. He was a thirty-something man named Anapa, which he explained to Adam meant the Sparkling Sea. He also served as their jeep driver, which seemed to require a sharper eye and greater ability to make swift decisions than flying a helicopter as there was one road on the island, unpaved, unreliable, and when it climbed up into the hills, downright dangerous.

Rangiroa, Bill explained to Adam, was a thin, forty-two mile long atoll surrounded by a turquoise lagoon, which in turn was surrounded by the mighty Pacific. It was sparsely populated, and there were no towns or roadway stands or palm-thatched shops, Adam couldn't help noticing, always having his eye out for boutiques where he might find amenities or souvenirs, touristy things. There were slim pickings here. Occasionally he would see some trash and fences, but those were the only signs of man's existence.

"There's a bird sanctuary on Motu Paio," Anapa explained. "It's very famous."

"I wish we had time to see it. Only not today," Bill advised him.

"And Rangiroa also is known for its sharks. We have three or four varieties. And giant manta rays."

Adam didn't know whether to say Yay or Boo-hoo. As far as he was concerned, this would be the perfect spot to build a penal colony, a new Devil's Island, surrounded as it was by sharks, manta rays, birds, and whatever else lurked among the coconut palms. It was a prison that didn't need any barbed-wire fences. Bill said he'd brought him here to show him something, but what could it possibly be?

The jeep was cutting its own path now through a forest of tropical jungle. The air was thick with mosquitoes. The wheels kept getting stuck in nests of big rotting coconuts, hundreds of them. Adam thought they must be in the center of the island, sunless, damp, and hot.

Suddenly the jeep pulled to a stop in front of a big stone house set back in the thickets with a long terrace that overlooked the sea. Bill and Anapa led the way up onto the terrace and Adam followed suit.

"Well, this is it, I've rented it," Bill announced. "It has to be built up and modernized but that's all part of the deal. And in French Polynesia, after you rent a place for five years, you're allowed to buy it."

Adam stared at the gigantic shell of a huge empty stone house, which he supposed at one time had been a livable dwelling.

"You and I can have it all redone, I have the money to do it up just the way we did our apartment by the High Line," Bill reassured him. "Have a swimming pool put in. Modern appliances." He climbed up on the long terrace that faced the sea. "Look at this view. Of the setting sun over the Pacific. It's the best vista I've ever seen anywhere in my life."

"And it never changes," Anapa reassured them. "The sunset looks the same every night three hundred and sixty days a year."

"Three hundred and sixty-five days, you mean," Adam said. "No, there will be five days with bad weather. Can't be helped."

"Oh."

"Can you picture it?" Bill asked. "Just the two of us? Every night on this terrace, holding each other, how romantic it will be." He put his arm around Adam's waist. "Don't worry, Anapa knows about us."

Anapa smiled and moved a discreet distance away.

"It's like we've come to the end of the earth," Bill said.

"Or that the end of the earth has come to us," Adam said.

"Don't you like it here, darling?"

"In my opinion, this would take some getting used to."

Before they started their flight back to Bora Bora, Bill thought Adam should see the beach, even swim a bit in the calm ocean waters. Anapa drove them down to the edge of a promontory where there was a gorgeous swath of white sand and crystal clear turquoise water that was softly lapping its way onto it. Adam, his brain in a fog, started to wade out into the ocean but fist-sized chunks of broken coral made it hard for him to make his way and he turned back.

"Bill, you have to be out of your ever-lovin' mind," he said.

ADAM AND BILL LAY on the outdoor terrace of their Bora Bora bungalow as the sun began sinking over the far reaches of the lagoon. They both wore sunglasses. And white swim trunks. They lay together listening to the water lapping against the steps that descended into the lagoon and enjoying the warm ocean breeze as it rippled seductively over their bodies.

Finally Adam said, "Bill, I've been thinking about what we're going to do when we get back to New York."

"Hmm ..."

"Are you listening?"

"Yes."

Adam continued, "Since you've come out of the closet, at least in Bora Bora, that means a whole new world has opened up for you. It means you might as well come out in New York as well and explore your options there."

"What did you have in mind?"

"Why not ask Miranda to cook up a reality show based on the two of us, you know, a famous ex-soap opera star living with his lover right on the High Line? You're a well-known TV celebrity, after all. A cable channel might pick it up or a Netflix or Amazon might want to stream it. The show could follow us through our first years of marriage, starting with us making plans for our wedding, then having the actual ceremony itself on the High Line, then follow our lives as we take your past success as a soap star into unchartered territory and get involved in new, exciting projects."

"Adam, I always wondered if deep down you didn't harbor a desire to step into the limelight yourself somehow. Now my question's been answered."

Adam was genuinely hurt. He took his sunglasses off and turned on his side and stared at Bill. "I never interfered with your career, never tried to overshadow you in any way. I supported you completely which was the right thing to do. It's only now that your soap has come to an end that I'm speaking up. Why won't you consider my idea at least, for both our sakes?"

Now it was Bill's turn to take his sunglasses off and stare into Adam's eyes which were a beautiful deep sea blue. "Because we're giving up the bright lights and the hurdy gurdy for a peaceful existence on Rangiroa, just the two of us. I'm not going back to the rat race."

Sighing, Adam got up and said, "I feel like a swim." He started down their private steps leading into the calm waters of the lagoon just as their fellow bungalow dweller Lewis Blackwater passed by on the boardwalk.

Lewis called out, "Oi, young Adam! I'd be careful if I were you, going in the water just as evening's coming on. It's when the small blacktipped reef sharks come close to shore."

"Thanks for the warning."

Adam climbed back up the steps and went inside the bungalow leaving Bill to finish sunbathing alone.

Adam stood over the glass floor panels in the middle of their exclusive living area through which he could see the lagoon floor below him, beautiful coral formations where delicate reef fish darted. Only now Adam knew that he needed to look more closely at the wondrous seascape that surrounded him. Among the brightly colored fishes, he could make out the tentacles of the poisonous sea anemone and noticed a few of the prehistoric looking moray eels, snail-like coral dwellers, slithering on the bottom of the ocean floor, blending in with the sand. He'd read they were very aggressive and could bite your finger off if the mood struck them. And there were probably barracudas sharpening their teeth somewhere nearby and puffer fish too. If you accidently brushed up against one, it could swell up like a volleyball with a hundred sharp spikes embedded in it and attack. It wasn't all about the adorable sea turtles everybody talked about but that he had yet to spot, or the energetic dolphins that didn't even come close to shore.

When Bill came in from sunbathing, Adam turned to him and said, "You know something, I'm exhausted from fighting Paradise itself." Then he went to take a nap.

Adam's obvious discontent hit Bill in the gut. He couldn't understand how anybody given the chance to trade the trials and tribulations of the fast life for a worry-free existence far from its illusory excitement wouldn't jump at the chance. And then the truth hit him. It was their age difference that he'd somehow deluded himself into thinking wouldn't come into play in their generally compatible relationship. Bill had already enjoyed a life of glamorous drama but Adam hadn't. It was only natural that he would want to try to have one for himself. Bill had hoped the idea of just being with him would provide enough satisfaction. Apparently, it didn't.

Bill tried one last stab at making Adam appreciate the sweetness of the tranquility that was available to him here in the islands. He ordered a canoe-delivered dinner to be set up on their private terrace where they could dine alone under the moonlight and the thousands of stars that flooded the sky. But Adam only picked at his food disappointedly. He'd rather have gone by shuttle to a restaurant in town and walked around a bit after their meal. But he didn't admit it to Bill as the canoe-delivered dinner had been a thoughtful gesture. Yet with each bite he thought with a kind of desperation about how they would be dining every night on the terrace of that heavy block of a house in the jungles of Rangiroa. And that his youth would slowly be drained away with each passing sunrise and sunset and that he might as well stuff his dreams in a bottle and toss them into the waves where they would drift away on some thoughtless current to who knows where. And that before he knew it he would be old, without his youth and without his dreams, eventually burying Bill in a jungle plot on Rangiroa and spending the rest of his years there alone, just waiting to die himself.

"It's a delicious dinner, isn't it?" Bill asked. "They have a great chef here."

Adam smiled. "I'd give him three-and-a-half stars at least but I couldn't give him four in good conscience as the chicken's a bit overcooked."

"I'd have to agree with your assessment."

That night Adam couldn't sleep. He was restless and agitated.

"You're keeping me awake with all that tossing and turning," Bill complained.

"Sorry. What time is it?"

"Nearly midnight."

Adam sat straight up in bed. "I know. Let's go for a midnight dip. We'll stay close to our bungalow and look up at the stars."

"Really?" Bill, who'd been grumpy about not being able to get to sleep, suddenly came very much alive and said, "Well, why not? Those blacktipped reef sharks our limey friend Mr. Blackwater warned us about no doubt swam back out to sea after sunset."

"I'm sure they did and I'm not afraid of any of them anymore, anyway," Adam advised him. They slipped into their trunks and went out onto the terrace.

"Let's not wake the neighbors," Bill warned. His voice seemed to echo all the way across the lagoon and come back to him. "It's so quiet here!"

They descended into the inky water by way of their terrace steps and dog paddled a foot or two away from them. The ocean was warm and the night breezes fresh. A full moon was up in the sky, and they could make out the craters and crevices on its surface almost as clearly as if they'd been looking at it through a telescope. They watched a shooting star as it plunged from the sky toward the ocean.

"I'm glad we came out here," Bill said. "They say you can see loads of shooting stars each night but of course we're usually asleep so I can't personally confirm that."

"Hold me," Adam said and Bill pulled him in close and they kissed—a long, deep, romantic kiss. When Adam drew back, he murmured, "I can't. I can't stay here."

Bill paddled away and climbed back up the steps where he sat down on the terrace, hugging his knees and staring off into space. Adam sat down beside him feeling guilty but resolute.

"I was waiting for that," Bill said. "And you didn't disappoint me."

Adam touched Bill's cheek. "Won't you come back to New York and stay with me for good? Can't we have our life's adventure there instead of in Tahiti?"

Bill said, "I have to admit that it wasn't just your tossing and turning that was keeping me awake. I couldn't fall asleep because of the whirring going on in my own mind. I was thinking of how to answer you when you asked that question. Adam, I'm going to stay here in Bora Bora and go on from here to Rangiroa. Why should I even return to New York just to turn around and fly back?

I can have my belongings packed up and shipped to me here." He took Adam's hand in his and rubbed it gently. "I hope you'll stay with me."

"No, I'm going back," Adam said. "I'm going to put together a reality show with or without you."

"I admire your gumption," Bill said, laughing sadly. "I recognize it. I had some of it too in my day. I'll continue to pay the rent, of course, and you can keep using our joint bank account until you have something set up for yourself and feel secure."

"Thanks, Bill. I really love you, you know."

"I do know. And I love you."

Adam remembered the shooting star they'd just seen fall into the sea and wondered if it didn't represent Bill's path. Bill was somehow done with life as Adam knew it. Adam liked to think that an ascending firework being shot up into the sky represented his path.

Bill disappeared into the bungalow and, relieved to have settled things, though not in the way he'd have preferred, lay down on their big double bed and fell asleep.

Adam stayed out on the terrace for a while and had a good cry, realizing how much Bill loved him and how much he loved Bill, but also how much he hated the islands that made up the so-called windward group of French Polynesia.

ADAM RAN INTO MAX'S girlfriend Celina on the High Line.

"You look spiffy," she told him. "Is that sweater you're wearing cashmere?"

"It is." He'd paid a king's ransom for a white cashmere sweater at Brooks Brothers.

"And a pair of fitted gray gabardine trousers and gray calfskin leather dress shoes," she noted. "I'm impressed."

"I'm off to an important meeting at the Pearl Hotel."

"I see. I'm afraid I've had my fill of those," Celina said.

Adam blushed, he didn't know exactly why. "But your singing career is taking off. I see your name lots of different places."

"Beginner's luck, nothing more. Anyway, I have some shopping to do. Dazzle them at your important meeting, Mr. Brooks Brothers."

"I plan to."

Adam was joining Miranda Schule at the outdoor restaurant on the roof of the Pearl Hotel for lunch. Even though it was late September, it hadn't closed yet for the season, probably because of the fine weather, still in the upper sixties. Nearly every table was filled. When Adam arrived he saw Miranda had already staked her claim at one of the prime poolside tables. She waved him over, gave him a peck on the cheek while he complimented her on her appearance, even though he thought she was overdressed in a brown suede suit and matching handbag, was wearing too much makeup, and that her red hair swept up in a bun resembled a tuft of cotton candy. The executive look, he supposed.

"I haven't seen you since our dinner right here in the summer when I had to give Bill the bad news," she remarked.

"I remember that evening."

"Of course it didn't turn out to be bad news, did it? How could retiring to Tahiti have a downside to it?"

"It couldn't," he mumbled.

"I'll say not," she agreed. "That's my dream. To be able to afford to retire to someplace like that. But first you have to be willing to put in quite a few hours with your nose to the grindstone. Which I'm prepared to do."

"Yes," Adam said eagerly. "So am I."

"What are you having for lunch?" she asked him.

"I'll have whatever you recommend," he said.

"Well, really, I can't recommend anything. I've never had lunch here before and I'm not the waiter. You're on your own."

Confused, he daydreamed for a moment, remembering that movie star Julienne Hughes and her hot boyfriend in his skintight bathing suit that showed his package to perfection. They'd sat at the table next to them that night Miranda had given Bill and Tandy the ax. No doubt she was making a new movie somewhere far away and falling into that stud's arms every night.

"Adam," Miranda nudged him as the waiter appeared. "I'll have the same as you."

They settled on two seafood platters and two iced teas.

"No alcohol for me," she insisted. "It depletes that energy I absolutely depend on. Since becoming an independent producer, I've found that hunting down the right property is a twenty-four hour job. I wake up every night and jot down ideas. Not that ideas alone are enough. I'm a results-oriented person."

"I know you are. And you've chosen an exciting career."

She sighed. "Adam, you're making me trot out the old chestnut. *I didn't choose it. It chose me.*"

"Of course."

As they ate, Miranda wanted Adam to do all the talking. "Tell me about the South Pacific."

He painted a rosy picture of morning swims among twisting corals and fluorescent fishes, trips to unexplored outer reef islands, romantic dinners delivered by canoes, and ever-blowing trade winds and sunsets that had no parallel anywhere in the modern world.

"Then why'd you leave?" she asked as she finished her seafood and dabbed her lips with a linen napkin.

Adam swept his hands dramatically toward the Manhattan skyline. "For this," he said. "It's an even more compelling landscape."

"You're the one able to compare them."

Adam had texted her his idea for the reality series he had in mind. The episodes would follow him, Adam Marsh, as he hunted for the perfect husband. He would date lawyers, architects, bankers, entertainers. But the hook for this series was that all the candidates had to live along the High Line and in each episode Adam would visit them in their trendy apartments. The audience would get to weigh in on how the apartments could be redone for the newlyweds as well as vote for Adam's husband to be. But, of course, he'd have the final say as to who he'd marry. But would take their votes into consideration. In the final episode, Adam would marry the lucky winner in a publicized wedding on the High Line with famous guest singers and dancers performing against spectacular backdrops.

"What did you think of my proposal?" he asked enthusiastically.

"It had some interesting things in it," she said. "Its success would really boil down to the way it was done. Its style. You know, it would need to visually knock everybody's socks off, that kind of thing?"

"Exactly," Adam agreed. "It has to be cutting edge. You'd need the right people working alongside you."

"Well, that's just it," Miranda said, "and please don't take this the wrong way, but what right people are waiting to work alongside you? You're an unknown. How could you expect to attract an audience in the first place?"

Adam stuttered, "Publicity. Somebody who knows what they're doing, planting stories in all the right places."

Miranda shook her head. "That's a lot to ask somebody to do when you don't have one press clipping of your own to pull out of your dresser drawer. Now Bill, he's a different story, he's a known factor already. He might have a chance to pull something like that off." She lowered her voice. "You know, I miss that man. I was cleaning out my old office at the studio the other day and I noticed a framed photograph of the three of us together on the set, Tandy Marlowe, Bill and me, sitting on Dr. Grange's desk in his East Hampton study. We were all laughing at nothing in particular. It made me long for the old days." Miranda shook her head. "Sorry, Adam, I'll have to pass on developing your series idea. They say there's no new material out there, no fresh plot lines and, as it turns out, I've got something very much like your story in development already. Only it's from a woman's perspective which I think makes a lot more commercial sense than coming from a gay man's point of view. I have a well-known actress in mind for it so I have a decent chance to sell the thing. It's remarkably like your idea, actually. A reality show where a woman hunts for a successful husband among men who live in exclusive properties in Chelsea and winds up tying the knot right on the High Line in front of a crowd of enthusiastic strangers. It's called *Lady in Waiting*. But maybe that title's too old fashioned. I should call it *Her Cutting Edge*."

Adam bit his tongue. It was painfully obvious Miranda had ripped off his idea. Just now. And that she could get away with it. He pawed mindlessly at his new cashmere sweater.

"But," she said, "don't get discouraged. I'd still be glad to look at anything else you'd like to show me."

"I bet."

"Why don't you develop something that would include Bill? Like the two of you moving to Tahiti and exploring life together there? That's a wonderful slice of reality for you and it just might fly with your affluent gay audience. Think about it."

Adam forgot about it, but quick. He forgot about everything and that night he treated himself to a drunken binge in a Hell's Kitchen watering hole he used to haunt. He found himself an average-looking middle-aged man who'd just lost his job and was coming off a divorce and they had sex all night long in Adam and Bill's double bed.

The man left late in the day, and Adam, with a hangover, and in his bathrobe, his hair disheveled, stumbled out on his balcony with a cup of strong coffee and planted himself at the little table. Max and Celina were down in the garden below, sweeping the first of the falling leaves into a bag.

"When's Bill coming back?" Max called up to him.

That must be a trick question. They'd seen the guy he'd slept with leave their apartment. That must be it. And now he was being called to account.

Adam said breezily, "He's not. He's made an informed decision to stay forever in a tropical paradise. As for me, I'm going to be producing a reality show about my own life here in Chelsea. I want to get the first episode up and running before somebody gets the jump on me."

"Ambitious," said Max who pictured Adam hanging out his front window languidly watching the world go by.

Adam added, "Oh, Celina, I wonder if I could convince you to make a guest appearance in my show?"

"What would I do?"

"I could introduce you as my upstairs neighbor who just happens to be a singer. You could perform one of your songs, if you'd like, with the garden as the backdrop."

"It's nice to know someone's still thinking about my music."

Max stiffened.

"I'll think it over," she said icily, staring at Max who stopped sweeping and returned her icy stare.

So, they were quarreling about something. Adam wasn't in the head space to want to find out what it was all about. He stood up, deciding it was a good moment to go back inside. "Well, think my offer over," he called down to Celina.

"I will, but I have to say I don't think so."

"Yes, well ..." Adam said. "If you change your mind ..."

"Thank you." Then she turned her attention to Max and said, "I had to start from scratch. I didn't have the benefit of inheriting money from my parents like you did." Adam thought, ah-ha, suspicions confirmed. "Every gig I've scored, I've done the hard way, shed my blood, sweat, and tears with no help from anybody else."

Adam couldn't wait to get inside where he could concentrate on his creative ideas in the peacefulness of his own living room. To hear couples arguing was unpleasant to say the least. He shut the sliding door but peered down into the garden one last time. Celina stormed away from Max, back into the apartment building, slamming the door behind her. Adam closed his eyes. When couples walked away from each other ... when things fell apart ... it created an empty space in each of them that hadn't been there before. He knew from experience.

BILL LAY DAYDREAMING IN his hammock on the terrace of his house in the wilds of Rangiroa. Reveling in a tropical breeze, he stared out past a pleasing jungle of palm and coconut trees at the calm Pacific Ocean, imagining that Adam was a passenger on a steamer fast approaching the island. He closed his eyes and pictured Adam climbing up the steps to the terrace, setting his bags down and tiptoeing over to Bill and tapping him on the shoulder.

"I've come home," Adam said.

Bill smiled and said aloud, "I knew you'd come. I was expecting you."

"How's that?" came a voice behind him.

Startled, Bill turned around to find a sunburnt, wizened man with a long gray beard staring down at him. He was dressed in an ill-fitting pair of baggy shorts and a faded Hawaiian shirt.

"Excuse me," Bill said. "Who are you?"

"Your neighbor. It took me a while to get up enough courage to come say hello."

Bill got out of the hammock and shook the man's hand. "I'm Bill Cooly."

"John Martin."

"Well, Mr. Martin, it's a pleasure to meet you," Bill said, sizing him up as the type who'd chucked the harried life to sail the seas in his schooner before opening a beach bar to enjoy his golden years in Paradise. "You're my neighbor then?"

"Yes. I live in a hut a mile down the road. I've seen you coming and going."

Bill wanted to ask, "Did you just say a hut?" but thought better of it. Instead, he offered his unexpected visitor a beer.

"No. I don't accept favors I can't return," John Martin said gravely.

"It's no trouble. Really. I don't expect any reciprocation."

John Martin waved off his offer with an elaborate hand gesture. He asked impatiently, "You got disillusioned with the world too, did you?"

The question caught Bill off guard. But he rebounded as best he could. "No, I just retired."

"Then we have something in common," Martin proclaimed. "I retired too. In 1969 when I was 22. I gave up my job delivering pizzas and taking night classes in cultural anthropology at UC Berkeley. I'd had it with the threat of the Cold War ... realizing that the human race was essentially doomed and that it was only a matter of time before China or Russia dropped an atom bomb on California. And I didn't want to be around when they did. Hell, the establishment was bullshit anyway, soulless and corrupt, and the only things the counterculture offered in the way of an alternative were flowers and rock and roll. Well, I had a deep-seated conviction I could get an endless supply of flowers in a place like this and as it turned out I was right, and as for rock and roll, I figured, who needed it? Did you know when I caught a boat for Tahiti in August '69 the song they were playing over and over on the radio was *Polk Salad Annie*, the gator's got your granny? By some guy named Tony Joe White. It drove me crazy. It was the last song I ever heard and even now it's still rumbling around in my head. It's insistent. It's like a plague of sorts."

Bill sighed. *Why me?*

Martin continued, "I don't even know what the music is like nowadays."

"No," Bill said. "I don't imagine you would."

"During the past few days I made up my mind to come up here and ask you the question I've resisted asking anybody for forty-some years. What are they playing on the radio these days?"

Bill considered John Martin's earnest expression. It was mad, comical, and heartbreaking at the same time. Bill took a deep breath. Instead of humoring him, he said, "What's to tell? The world is still lacking and so is the music, I suppose. You haven't missed very much and yet you've missed everything."

John Martin threw him a shrewd look. "At least I've managed to cleanse myself of all the nonsense. Out here I've been able to hear myself think. And to finally understand who I am."

"You're very lucky." Bill thought it best to be short and to the point.

"Is it a matter of luck? Or is it because of the conscious decision I made to reject the constant static so that I could engage in right thinking?"

Bill couldn't believe it. He was actually standing on his terrace talking to a man who'd suffered some kind of mental breakdown, who was truly damaged. And he happened to be his closest neighbor. If it had only been Adam who'd tapped him on the shoulder. But it had been John Martin instead, a survivor from a nuclear bomb which a hostile superpower had forgotten to drop on Northern California but had exploded inside this man's brain anyway.

John Martin smiled and patted him on the back. "Well, I'll be going now. My brother."

Relieved, Bill said, "Yes. And you take care of yourself."

"If I don't, who will?"

And with that his neighbor was off.

Bill walked inside his empty house and shut the door behind him. He felt abysmally alone. He thought of the insanity he'd endured on the set of his soap, the in-fighting, the power plays, his desperate need to stay on top, his laser-like preoccupation with keeping his fan base at all costs. But civilization didn't have a monopoly on insanity. It was in every corner of the world, just down the road from him, under every rock, in every ocean wave, in every perfect sunset.

It was one of those moments you see in the movies, Adam thought, the ones that are never supposed to happen in real life. He'd been standing at the kitchen window drinking a cup of tea with steamed milk when he noticed a cab pulling up to the curb and a man in a dark overcoat with a suitcase getting out. Curious to know who he was, and, frankly, whether or not he was good looking, Adam gave him more than a passing glance. The man set his suitcase on the sidewalk and, under buckets of rain, shielded his eyes and gazed up at Adam in the window. It was Bill.

Adam was amazed. He took a fortifying last sip of tea and pulled the window up and leaned out. The rain soaked him but he didn't care. "You've had one too many sunsets, is that it?" he shouted down.

"What's that?" Bill called up.

"I said, come up and join me for a cup of tea! Don't just stand there like a statue!"

Adam felt ripples of excitement running through him as he quickly checked himself out in the mirror while he thought with relief how a law student from NYU he'd met on Grindr had turned down his invitation to come by and have sex with him today because he was too busy studying for exams. Sometimes disappointments turned out to be blessings in disguise.

He threw himself onto the white leather sofa and struck a casual pose while he listened to the key turn in the lock. Then he watched as his estranged husband-to-be walked through the door looking like a drowned rat with a very sexy suntan.

"Hello, stranger," Adam said. "Back for a visit?"

"Huh-uh. Back to stay." Bill grinned a sheepish grin.

Adam was nonplused. "Why?" he asked. "What happened?"

"You can't guess?"

Adam was incredulous. "Really? You missed me?"

"Oh, I don't know about you," Bill teased him. "I missed New York, though."

Adam made tea for him and heated some scones which he carefully arranged on a plate and set on the kitchen table as Bill took a hot shower.

Bill came into the kitchen wearing a fluffy blue cotton robe, toweling his hair dry, very much at ease. He found Adam sitting at the large wooden table, his hands crossed, staring at him expectantly.

"May I?" Bill sat down opposite him. Adam nodded.

Bill laughed as he spread some lemon curd on a scone. "Our Brit friend, Mr. Blackwater, would approve of us having a civilized tea, I'm sure. Remember him? The bird watcher and nature enthusiast?"

"Yes, of course. He warned me about the reef sharks coming in to feed at our bungalow at sunset. Good thing he did, come to think of it, as I'm probably alive today because of his warning. Ever see him again?"

"No ... I was alone on Rangiroa. I never went back to Bora Bora. Oh, I shouldn't really say I was alone. Turns out I had a fascinating neighbor I never knew existed until he showed up at my place one day as I was napping in my hammock. He was stark raving. He'd left the States because the Russians were trying to drop a nuclear bomb on him."

"We've always had our share of eccentric neighbors it seems."

"What's going on around here?"

"There's a negative vibe in this place at the moment with our dependable landlord and his girlfriend, but I'll fill you in later. Don't you have jet lag? You must be exhausted."

"I crashed one night in Honolulu and one in L.A. So let me put it this way. It would be a perfect afternoon to spend in bed. Wouldn't you agree?"

Adam felt guilty. He looked down at his folded hands. Bill obviously hadn't slept with anybody since they'd parted. He, on the other hand, well ... But it hadn't been a barrel of laughs to pick up strangers with nothing to show for it in the end.

"Your project?" Bill said, spreading lemon curd on his second scone. "It's coming along?"

Adam gazed into his eyes. Then he got up and knelt on the floor beside Bill. "It's been a total failure," he admitted.

"I'm sorry, Adam."

"Give my hair a muss up, like you used to," Adam asked him.

"All right."

Adam lay his head on Bill's leg and Bill ran his fingers thoughtfully through Adam's hair. "The truth is," Adam said, "I've missed you more than I thought possible. Only I didn't let myself think about it much. I've had a pretty rough go of it and if I'd dwelled on how the two of us broke up ... I'd have crumbled. I'm glad you've come home."

LOUISE, DON'T GO

"HAVE YOU SEEN THE other American lady who's staying with us?"

Alice Thompson lowered her cup into the saucer and with some confusion met the eyes of the head waiter. "No ..." she answered slowly. "I don't believe I have."

"She's a retired schoolteacher like you, miss. She's been here two or three days. Funny your paths haven't crossed, especially since there aren't many guests this time of year."

Alice pulled her shawl around her shoulders to deflect the March wind that was somehow blowing right through the windowpane behind her. The window was tightly bolted, there were no cracks in the glass, no splits in the wood, yet the teacup was quivering, leaves of a discarded book were turning, and she felt an iciness in her bones.

"Shall I light a fire?"

"No, John, don't bother. I'll be going upstairs soon." To light a fire on such a bright and shining day, when the hillsides were already covered with blue and white wildflowers, seemed foolish.

Alice watched the sun speckle the potted palm, secure in its copper urn, the centerpiece of the Braemar Hotel drawing room. Circling the palm were clusters of well-worn armchairs and tables set for afternoon tea. But for the moment, Alice had the drawing room all to herself, so she felt at ease to give her face a quick, unobserved touch-up. Holding her pocket mirror at arm's length, she applied some rouge to her cheeks and dabbed some powder on her nose. By just slightly turning the mirror, she was able to see branches of a willow tree scraping against the window. Its blossoms were white and ripe.

She made her way up the steep wooden stairs, dark even in all the sunshine, to her room on the second floor. She had left her detailed map of Scotland open on the bed, and staring at it now she felt that, all its crags and crannies considered, Scotland was a large and unfamiliar place, and she had barely begun her exploration.

She had marked her route with a red pen, carefully circling the towns and villages she had already visited and connecting them with red arrows. She had traveled down from Aberdeen to Edinburgh, over to Perth, to Peebles, and up into the middle of the Grampian Range, to the Highland town of Braemar. With satisfaction, she removed her red pen from her purse and circled BRAEMAR. After several more days here, she would travel on to the Hebrides, then down the coast, winding back east to Glasgow.

Outside her second-floor window were the glacier-formed Grampians, still holding some snow. The sun, though it was early afternoon, seemed already to be making its descent, sinking almost imperceptibly into the white.

Alice pulled the pleated curtain across the window and felt her way in the dimness to the edge of the bed. Her fingers fumbled for the map and when they closed around it, they paused, and instead of removing it, they lifted it gingerly, and Alice slid under the oversized map as if it were a blanket. She was too tired to fold it back up, too tired to fetch the wool comforter from the bottom of the bureau drawer, too tired to do anything but sleep.

Her nap lasted only forty minutes, yet on waking she was refreshed. When she pulled back the curtain, the theater of mountains lay before her, just as she had left them less than an hour ago, just as they had prevailed for ages.

It was as she was returning from her afternoon walk, strolling down the path that led from a deserted farmhouse back to the hotel, that she met Louise Montrose.

"It looks like heather, doesn't it, but I suppose it's a bunch of ragweed."

Alice studied the sickly purple buds that the other woman proffered. "Heather blooms in August and September. I can't imagine what you've got there."

Louise laughed. "I'll settle for ragweed. I thought I had a bit of the naturalist in me. I'm beginning to find out it's a very little bit. Staying at the hotel?"

"Yes."

"How about joining me for tea?"

"It would be a pleasure."

"So, you finally met." John grinned at Alice and Louise as they came in from the winding path through the back door.

Alice nodded. "Yes. You said it was bound to happen."

"It's the first I heard of this inevitable rendezvous," Louise quipped. "But why not?"

In the drawing room, half a dozen guests were gathered. There was Signor Rossi, an Italian textile merchant who commuted back and forth between Milan and the Highlands and came regularly to this hotel for a spot of relaxation. There was a quiet family from New Delhi who kept to themselves, and an older American doctor from Long Island who'd left his family back in the States to get in touch with his Scottish roots and do some hiking. John McAlister, as he had done for the past twenty-five years, made his way around the room, unobtrusively, offering tea sandwiches, scones, and jam to the guests.

Alice and Louise took their tea by the window where Alice had sat the previous afternoon. John had been on the mark. Almost at once, they discovered some surprising facts. They were both American schoolteachers who had retired four years ago, had taught the fourth grade for the same number of years, forty to be exact, and within a hundred miles of each other, Alice in Portsmouth, Ohio, and Louise in Vincennes, Indiana.

"This is all very funny," Louise chuckled. "I've had to come all the way to a spot in the Scottish Highlands to meet a kindred spirit who was only a hundred miles away for the last forty years, is that it?"

"I'm afraid so. But life is full of little ironies and surprises."

Louise, less given to fanciful insights than Alice, blurted, "And what about our ages? I'm sixty-nine."

"Seventy," Alice stated emphatically.

Louise brightened. "I'm willing to let you have that extra year. How are you getting around?"

"Well, by train ... and then by bus or hired car."

"I have a rental car. I've treated myself to one of these new Volkswagen Beetles. It was expensive but it's my only luxury treat—maybe ever." She laughed heartily. "I picked it up in Glasgow. It was the only one they had."

Alice had no idea what a Volkswagen Beetle was. She had never even learned to drive.

"I'll tell you what," Louise continued. "We can take some excursions together. How about it?"

"It would make a nice change. I usually stay put. I may not look it but I'm a bit of a walker, I did bring along a pair of hiking shoes."

"Waterproof boots were the first thing I packed."

"Are you sure you wouldn't mind?" Alice asked tentatively.

"What? The company?"

Alice nodded.

"Just the tonic for me."

So, it was settled. They'd take a drive tomorrow.

Though they shared similar backgrounds, the two women would have struck most people as being very different—Louise, heavy, commanding, with a low, raspy voice, and Alice, slightly frail, with tentative movements and a pleasing shyness in her speech.

"This your first time at this hotel?" Louise asked, spreading blackberry jam on a warm scone.

"Yes. And you?"

"My first stay too. Only it's so damn familiar. I seem to turn corners knowing what's around the bend. I've had acquaintances who've stayed in the Highlands before. Maybe one of them was a guest at this very hotel and described it to me."

"That must be it," Alice agreed.

Louise wrapped a scone in a tissue. "This will make a perfect midnight snack."

That night Alice wished she'd had the wherewithal to wrap a scone for later as she was still awake at midnight reading Sir Walter Scott's *The Bride of Lammermoor*. Well, not exactly reading it, but holding it open while her mind drifted through the past.

She thought about how times had changed so dramatically over the past forty years when she'd first started teaching in 1913. Her salary had been over twenty dollars a week but when she retired last Christmas, she was making a hundred dollars a week. When she first walked into her fourth-grade class, Woodrow Wilson had been president; when she walked out, Dwight Eisenhower was weeks away from his inauguration. And here in the United Kingdom, Queen Elizabeth was no longer Princess Elizabeth but preparing for her coronation this coming June 1953, the first time a coronation would be televised. Back in Portsmouth, the shoe manufacturer Ellis Johnson and his family, in the comfort of their mansion in the wealthy enclave of Boneyfiddle, would surely be watching it on their color television. They could afford one, Alice reasoned, even though a color television cost over a thousand dollars ...

A thousand dollars ... two-and-a-half-months' salary for her when she retired ... Alice quietly drifted into a haunted dream about Lucy Ashton's tragic love affair with Edgar Ravenswood, as Scott's novel slipped from her grasp and fell onto the floor.

As they drove on the meandering road, Louise had to honk as she turned each bend, to drive the sheep back onto the hillsides.

"They've got to understand we have the right of way. We don't want any collisions."

"They're so sweet and trusting," Alice said.

"They are that."

As they passed a flock in a soft glen, the sheep seemed to stare at them complacently. "Why do some have pink dye on their wool and others blue?" Alice wondered.

"Markings. So the owners can tell which ones are theirs, I suppose. They'd make wonderful pets, wouldn't they? What would they say back in Portsmouth if you brought one home with you and kept it in the backyard?"

Alice laughed. "They'd probably shake their heads and say, 'Look at our schoolteacher now. She's finally gone over the edge.'" She suddenly turned her head up to the cloudless, shiny sky. Portsmouth, Ohio, was a faraway blur. There was so much distance between them now. She could hear the rush of the great Ohio River, but that was all.

Louise parked outside the gates of Balmoral Castle, the Queen's summer residence, but it would presumably be some months before any royal blood arrived, certainly not until after the coronation at least. And it wasn't open for visitors until next month. Louise had a little trouble squeezing her ample frame out of the compact VW, but Alice, with the spirit and energy of a young girl, nearly flew from the car to press her nose to the iron gates.

"Louise, it's so magnificent! It really is!" She ignored the curses of her companion who, huffing, strode up behind her.

"Give me a minute to catch my breath." Louise, brushing a wayward strand of thick, reddish-brown hair off her forehead, opened a pair of miniature binoculars and scanned the facade of the imposing castle. "Not much going on in there, I can tell you that."

"Oh, may I see?"

"I was kidding you, Alice. There are too many trees placed at well-thought-out intervals to prevent anybody getting a clear view across that great lawn into any of the windows."

"You mean some landscaper would have gone to such trouble?"

"Probably. Acting on royal orders some time ago. You see, the trees are arranged too perfectly, symmetrically, like men on a chessboard."

At any rate, the dark branches crisscrossed, hundreds of pairs of skeletal hands, palms thrust out, nature's natural curtain.

"A protector of privacy," Louise noted, almost disgruntled. "Typical." Then she added, "But we do have to protect our privacy, oh, yes."

"There's a clearer view at the end of the gates. There's a gazebo there and once in it, you've only got to peer over some short shrubs to get a good view." Alice's voice trailed off and she made no move, waiting for Louise's response.

Louise's response was a strange laugh and then a shrug. "You've never been here before, you say?"

"No." Then Alice began to stutter. "I did read up on Balmoral—"

"Must be some detailed guidebook you've got. And some memory. Let's go and see."

It was just as Alice had described. A round, oak wood gazebo afforded them a clear view through one of the largest windows in the closest turret. Louise had her binoculars up to her eyes in no time. "Somebody's moving in that window. It's a man in a long dark coat. He's pacing back and forth."

Alice nodded eagerly. "It must be a sentinel."

"Take a look." Louise handed her the glasses. Alice studied the figure slowly pacing. His hands, covered by white gloves, were clasped behind him.

"It's as if he's been doing this forever. Maybe waiting for someone or something."

"Summer, no doubt," Louise deduced. "Just like I am. In fact, I should have planned my trip for summer. I could have had a tour of the place. And the heather would have been in bloom."

Alice handed Louise her binoculars. "Louise, this is the perfect time for traveling. There are no crowds, and we have bracing, clear weather."

"You have something there. It's just that I've saved my pennies for this trip for such a long time and want to see everything possible."

Alice didn't reveal her secret. She hadn't had to save her pennies for this trip. But this wasn't the right moment to reveal that to Louise, who had saved hers just to enjoy moments like this. Instead, she said encouragingly, "Well, if you don't get to see everything this time, you'll be back again. Pennies have a way of mounting back up."

"But not my energy."

Alice disagreed. "Oh, no, that too." They walked back to the car.

As the afternoon light began to vanish, Louise put the gray sweater she was folding onto the bed and switched on the table lamp. But she couldn't wrest her eyes away from the window. Her room on the ground floor looked out the back onto a rocky, moss-filled hill that turned upward into a crag. Its trees were beginning to green, that kind of daredevil bright green that comes after a snow, and those blue and white wildflowers were pushing up from the stones which, at odd intervals, broke through the earth. She watched as the room slowly grew white and the crag took refuge in the dark twilight until all that was left to see was her own reflection in the window which the cozy room and night outside seemed to share equally.

Alice sat alone in the drawing room. She could hear the clatter of dishes in the kitchen and smell the spices of the cock-a-leekie soup that was simmering. On the mantle was an old radio, its black plastic covering newly shined, and out of its mouth came the sounds of a graceful minuet punctuated by the rigorous coughs of John McAlister who was clearing up after tea.

Gazing into her pocket mirror, with the minuet whispering in her ear, Alice patted her snowy white hair, still stiff from the spraying she'd given it an hour ago. How she would have liked to get a permanent, but she would probably have to wait until she got to Glasgow to find a proper beauty parlor.

John coughed again. He had been surprised to see her sitting by herself. "Would you like more tea, miss? There's a bit left."

"Oh, John, no thank you. I was just resting. This is such a pleasant room. I always gravitate towards it. "

"I'm glad it suits you." He moved away, past the lithe and ever present shadows of the palm fronds.

SITTING IN A ROCKING chair in Alice's room, Louise paged through the photograph album Alice had brought with her ... the one she brought along whenever she left the safe confines of Portsmouth.

Alice. So many poses and yet always the same, confused at being so content, so ladylike, and always the same hunch of the shoulders and hand on the hip, as if she were frightened of the camera's precision and honesty.

There was Alice on the riverbank, flanked by her two sisters, dressed tight to the neck as if for winter, though the sunburnt grass was streaming up around their ankles ... Alice in her classroom, chalk smudges on her collar, while on the blackboard the diagrammed sentence lost a few of its dangling participles to the camera frame ... Alice with her thirty children on the school steps, a couple of eager boys straining to lift an umbrella over her head ... and so on and on through the entire photograph album.

Louise nodded at the photographs from time to time, recognizing certain moments of her own life in many of them. She shut the album. "Thank you for sharing these memories."

"They are wonderful memories but all behind me now." She returned the album to her bureau drawer then studied her new friend a moment before admitting, "I know you had to save your pennies for this trip, but I didn't. The parents of the students I taught over the years came up with the money and presented me with a check for this trip at my retirement at Christmas. It was such a generous gesture. It warmed my heart to no end."

"Very generous. No such luck for me. Maybe because I was a bit of a hellion myself, more than a few of my fellow teachers, as well as the principal, were probably happy to see me finally go."

Alice laughed.

"But not the children," Louise confirmed. "We were buddies. They got a kick out of me, identified with my free spirit."

"Louise, have you ever been married?"

"Oh, yes."

Alice was shocked. She'd assumed ... assumed what exactly?

"Well, I haven't," Alice said. Then she realized what she'd assumed—that Louise was a spinster like herself, and, well, wasn't all that fond of men ... at least not enough to settle down with one. "Do you have children?"

"One son."

"I always felt guilty that I never had any."

"Guilty? That's a funny word to choose."

"But that's how I've always felt. Until now. You see, lately I realized I've had hundreds and hundreds of children, new ones year after year—and many of them remember me, even the ones grown up now with families of their own."

"My son was taken from me when he was eight," said Louise, seemingly out of the blue. "Bradley was his name. My ex-husband and his new wife got custody in court and moved to another town, I don't know where, and I never saw my son again."

"My," Alice said, her shoulders drooping, "can that happen?"

"It did happen. Bradley was taken from me because I had an unconventional life. A person I was seeing before and after I got married ... well, that person wasn't deemed acceptable in the eyes of society ... so my son was taken away from my sphere of influence ... that's what the court papers called it in the final judgment ... my 'sphere of influence' ... I wasn't allowed to contact my son again ... and all these years I agreed with that judgment, I felt I shouldn't contact him for his own sake ... but I'm not sure I was right about that ... but then, how do you ever know?"

Alice was at a loss for words. Bradley *was* his name, Louise had said, as if when he'd been taken from her by the court, he'd ceased to exist.

Louise continued, "It seemed inevitable for the times. 1925 in Vincennes, Indiana. Though I suppose nothing much has changed to this day. The court would still make that same judgment in 1953." Louise guffawed. "I sound pompous as hell stirring up my past mess at this point. I'll tell you something, I have a lot of living still to do, new places to see, new experiences to chalk up. A whole world is waiting for me and I'm going to meet it full on."

Alice beamed. "You're so right." She wanted to add something positive. "And teaching was so rewarding, wasn't it, all those years?"

"Without a doubt ..."

ALICE COULDN'T HELP STARING at the American doctor in the armchair across from her, gulping his morning tea. Instead of his usual corduroy jacket, he was wearing a plaid kilt. On his head was a glengarry, covering both his bald spot and the white curls that surrounded it.

He intercepted Alice's gaze and motioned for her to join him, but she smiled and politely declined. She was sure he was an erudite man, much like Signor Rossi, the textile merchant with whom she'd recently discussed the latest flooding of Venice and the peril to its vast treasures, but she couldn't see herself discussing coats of arms and Scottish lineage with the doctor when he looked like some whimsical aberration.

Her eyes drifted down to the map of Scotland in her lap, but the red pen in her hand could draw no further arrows, as anxious as it was to do so. The last town she'd circled was Braemar where she sat now. She knew she should be thinking about investigating new towns and valleys and lakes, but at the same time she felt curiously lax, her head spinning slightly. She was just plain tired … She'd put herself on an ominous schedule for a woman her age and it seemed to be catching up to her.

John McAlister had spotted the doctor, kilt and all, and was having trouble keeping a straight face. He exchanged a glance with Alice as he dusted the copper urn that held the palm.

"That palm is a fine specimen," Alice declared.

McAlister agreed. "I give it a little whiskey from time to time. It doesn't seem to mind."

"In fact, it flourishes."

The sun first caught the gold of the urn, then the gold of Alice's shoe buckles, then it rolled across the room in a wave as Louise came in to join them. "John McAlister, could you step into the hall with me for a minute? You too, Alice."

They followed her to the dark oil portrait of two men in heavy cloaks. It hung between the front door and the foot of the stairs. "Who are those men, anyway?"

John McAlister chuckled. "Curiosity got the better of you, eh?"

"Since I pass by these men several times a day, I thought I might as well know who I'm staring at."

"The gentlemen's names were John Freebairn and Rory McKay, neighbors and co-owners of this hotel at the turn of the century when they posed for this portrait. From what the folks in these parts say, the hotel was in its heyday when Freebairn and McKay ran it, not that it's doing too badly now. They had a reputation for being good business partners and were popular with everyone, even with the royals. In fact, Freebairn was quite the huntsman. From time to time, he'd bring venison, deer, or rabbits up to the gates of Balmoral Castle and leave his catch in the gazebo at the end of the front gates. He'd wave up to the sentry on duty in the castle to let him know he was leaving a present for whoever was staying there. Evidently, they were quite a pair, these men, and they loved this hotel."

Louise glanced quickly at Alice then back to the portrait. "Well," she said, "now I know a bit more about this history, I'll be sure to squirrel that knowledge away somewhere."

THE MIST IS ALWAYS there, the locals will tell you. You might think it's crept up on you, out of nowhere, on a late afternoon, but it's been in the air all along, fine and elusive, and you just didn't notice it. Maybe the sunshine diluted it or the snow obscured it, but take everything away and that's the one constant left.

Louise drove through the winding passes cautiously, climbing up around fifteen miles an hour when she dared. She was headed to the nature preserve of Morrone Birkwood where John McAlister had advised her there were lookouts that provided fantastic views of the Cairngorms mountain range. But her way ahead was blocked by the quick gathering fog.

Her passenger, Alice, literally sat on her hands so, though tempted, she wouldn't be able to reach over and switch off the ignition and bring the car to a halt. She bit her lip and stopped herself from insisting that Louise pull over. But pull over where? A grassy shoulder at the side of the road might be masking a sheer drop.

"I can't see a damn thing," Louise muttered.

"Well, that's obvious. I don't know what to do. Maybe you should let me out by the side of the road."

"Abandon you, just like that?"

"I'd at least be able to walk back and try to flag down somebody for help."

Then suddenly, on their left, a hazy sun began to burn a clear patch onto a meadow. "I've got visibility ahead now," Louise said, relieved.

"Thank the Lord," Alice sighed. "The weather here is so variable."

Louise edged the car to the side of a meadow and cut the engine. Not twenty feet away was the body of a sheep, its neck twisted, its hooves in the air as if trying to catch the sun and mist that flowed in alternating ribbons across the silent meadow.

"I wonder how long the poor thing's been dead." Louise stared blankly.

"I wish we hadn't seen it."

"That's the waste of a prayer, Alice."

"Yes ... you're right ... oh, I feel lightheaded ... I don't even remember where we were going ..."

"To the scenic overlook." But now even Louise wasn't sure. "Weren't we?"

"I couldn't say. I'm just so utterly tired ..."

"Try to relax then ... Just let yourself relax ..."

"I could almost fall asleep right here in the car."

"Well, go right ahead. I think I could do the same."

They had dreams ... small fragments of color ... threadlike movements of hands and faces—from the past ... even the sounds of a rushing river ... and then ... the smell of the night when all the perfume of the earth is at full strength. Then they woke up.

The meadow appeared before them, cold and green, even in early spring, and the dead sheep lay in such a way that it appeared to be stretching and sniffing the March air.

THE EVENING, FOLLOWING DINNER, as they were playing a game of checkers in the drawing room, Louise suddenly said, "I wonder after all if there is such a thing as death."

Alice looked up in amazement.

"Or death as we know it ... Take us for instance. I feel I've known you a lifetime, though we've only just met. I know, we've shared similar backgrounds and professions—but it's more than that. It's nothing I can rationalize, but from the beginning there was an immediate recognition, an understanding or shared feeling between us. When I looked through your album, I felt I knew more about you than the photographs revealed." Louise laughed. "Maybe we lived together in a past life. Maybe ... maybe we were even those two men in the portrait, John Freebairn and Rory McKay. You knew exactly where that gazebo was, just the spot Freebairn left his venison and waved up to the sentry in the window ... just like the sentry we watched through my binoculars. And this hotel is so familiar to me, though I don't know why." Alice began to protest but Louise cut her off and continued, "Maybe our lives have gone on and on through the centuries, linked together, reincarnated together, again and again."

"But Louise, there's no such thing."

"No," she said slowly. "No ... of course not." She shrugged. "But death ... I don't trust it..."

Alice seemed afraid and anxious to change the subject. "Let's see if we can get John McAlister to brew us a fresh pot of tea."

"Yes, nice and strong."

They were in luck. John hadn't retired for the night and obliged them with a Highland blend of black teas and some shortbread. Their hearts were no longer in the game. The red-and-black checkers, minutes ago vital adversaries, were now only a moderately interesting pattern on a faded checkerboard.

They took their tea with them as they walked together to the foot of the stairs.

"I'm planning to leave shortly after noon tomorrow," Louise abruptly declared. "It's a pity that we're heading in different directions, or I'd ask you to travel along with me."

Alice nodded. "You just came from the Hebrides and I'm excited about going there next. If only we'd met a little sooner, back in the Midwest, we could have coordinated our itinerary."

"Well, let's take a morning walk at least."

"Yes. Let's." Alice began to climb the stairs, holding her cup of tea straight out before her as if it were a flashlight.

"Don't spill," Louise cautioned.

"I'll be extra careful. Good night, Louise."

"Sleep well."

Alice dreamed that night, and in her dreams was the unmistakable scent of the earth which clung to her sheets and woke her in the morning.

BOTH THE STONE FARMHOUSE and the ruined wall surrounding it had become beautiful and serene with the lengthening of time. Weeds climbed into the broken windows and spiky yellow flowers nestled in the breaks of the circular wall.

The farmhouse consisted of one large room which was empty except for a splintered wooden table.

The two women stood in the silence of the room.

Louise broke the spell with, "This was the perfect place to come for our last walk."

Alice, overcome with emotion, replied, and her words echoed slightly around the stone walls, "Of course, you know what this reminds me of, don't you, Louise?"

"Certainly. Your old classroom. Our old classrooms. We couldn't have found a better spot to say goodbye. Not to mention the benefit that the farmhouse wasn't a long hike from the hotel."

Yet Alice was despairing. "I miss my old classrooms so. I feel untethered."

"The trick is not to look too hard for the past. Because it's not just a reminder of it in these stone walls or yellow flowers. It's inside us. I've decided to embrace my past and go and look for my son."

Cobwebs turned in the crystalline air, air filled with sun.

"Louise, I'm happy about that. But just be careful. It won't be easy."

"I'm not expecting it to be. I'm prepared to let the chips fall where they may." She nodded. "We'd better be getting back. I have some last-minute packing to do."

They made their way along the path, the same one on which they'd first met, this time passing an energetic Signor Rossi on a gentle incline.

"Anything of interest up that way?" he asked.

"Yes," Louise said. "A beautiful, abandoned old farmhouse. I don't think I'll forget it in a hurry."

"In that case, I would take great interest in seeing it," he answered and continued his walk more energetically than ever.

LOUISE LEFT EARLY THAT afternoon. Alice watched from her bedroom window as Louise, binoculars around her neck, refused John McAlister's assistance and lifted her few bags onto the back seat. Then she waved goodbye to John and, with a sweeping gesture, to the Grampians that glistened with melting snow. She idled her car down the driveway and turned onto the road to the east. A mist had come up and the car lost itself in the swirl, the red taillights fading away at last. And then all was mist.

Alice, suddenly panicked, rapped against the window and cried out, "No, Louise, don't go! ... Don't go!"

THE DRAWING ROOM WAS cold that night. But Alice, sitting alone in her chair by the mantle, didn't notice the numbness of her fingers, or even the symphony spurting from the old radio. She was thinking of Louise. Like a seer, she had felt a premonition of disaster as the car pulled away, but like the frail human being she was, she had allowed the car to disappear without any real protest. Exhaustion. It was in her eyes. Her smile. Her belly.

Tonight, the stairs swept upwards like the tiered cliffs of the Andes, never-ending, achingly steep. It took a lifetime to reach the top.

And her room was like a spinning hollow, filled with trees that parted to reveal hundreds of others. Her map lay carelessly open on the floor, but if she reached down to touch it, she would fall into it, be engulfed by the mountains and the broad valleys, and become webbed in by her own circles. And if she closed her photograph album on the top of her bureau, she would fall into that as well and be swallowed up by her own image, by the woman on the riverbank with her sisters, by the woman on the steps of the schoolhouse, a couple of eager boys straining to lift an umbrella over her head.

And the bed was like a starry night, with so much blackness, with so many stars to spare.

As her head touched the pillow, she knew she was dying. There was a bright pain within her that she had no will nor desire to stop.

There were human forms around her bed in a pale light.

Closing her eyes, she grabbed onto her fingers with such strength that she broke her bones. Life snapped from her.

Louise's car had gone off the road not ten minutes from the Braemar Hotel. It had gone off a short but steep incline and hit a lone tree in a meadow where a rushing stream came down a hillside. There was only the sound of the metal hitting the wood, and then the sound of splashing water. Louise had died instantly. But she wasn't found until later that night after the heavy mist had cleared.

It was summer's end. A Sunday. John McAlister listened to the sounds of far-off church bells that echoed through the mountains as he dusted the tables and brushed crumbs off the chairs when the hotel guests left after breakfast. The hotel was fully booked and that wouldn't change until the end of autumn.

Wispy quadrangles of sun moved into the drawing room. One of them spotlighted the palm and reminded him it was time to polish the copper urn.

As he rubbed on the polish with his soft flannel cloth, he was surprised to see two shiny black bugs sitting together, as if in communion, on one of the lower fronds. They had identical red dots on their lustrous backs although one was slightly smaller and appeared more tentative than the other.

Though he wasn't quite sure why, he was mesmerized by their presence, as if there was something about them that struck an odd note of familiarity. And he was a bit in awe at the way, with an almost single-mindedness of purpose, they began to climb, slowly, side by side, up the trunk of the palm.

BLONDS

HANK OPENED HIS LEGS, and between his suntanned thighs Provincetown Harbor was born. A precise miniature, a nature watercolor on a fan.

Sailboats made their way past the lighthouse toward the sea, a few red rocks still rose above the swelling tide, a gull circled slowly in the air. All this under the auspices of a molten sun. Though it was only ten in the morning, everything was a bitter white. Hank could hardly catch a breath.

Six-foot-four, with a wide chest and muscular arms, Hank overpowered the deck chair he was lying on. There was no room to keep his arms at his sides, so he let them dangle onto the wooden planks. The suntan oil he'd rubbed over his body was running in rivulets into his belly button and down his arms, making a sizzling sound when it dropped on the deck.

Because of the blinding sunlight, he kept his eyes shut most of the time, but occasionally he'd open them for a peek at the harbor between his thighs. It fitted so nicely there, the whole of the bay. It was soothing to know that even if he couldn't squeeze comfortably through every doorway or fit onto every piece of furniture, he had control over the entire landscape.

He heard the glass doors slide open, then the sound of bare feet thumping on the deck.

Opening his eyes, he found Erik kneeling at his feet. Had it been only one week that the boy had been here? They were so comfortable with each other, he'd already taken Erik's presence for granted and nearly lost track of time.

"No need to get up yet," Hank insisted.

"Ten o'clock already." The boy yawned. "Don't we have to go to Francisco's this morning?"

Hank shrugged. "I've got a hunch it might rain pretty soon. It's so humid. We'll probably have to postpone." He stroked Erik's cheek. "Why don't you go back in and try to get some more sleep? You could use it. We were playing poker till four in the morning."

"Then how come you're up so early?"

"That's just me."

"It's too hot to sleep. That's what woke me up. It was stifling."

"Not much better out here, baby ..."

Just beyond a kneeling Erik, Hank saw three young men drifting past the deck in an inner tube, splashing each other, panicking in jest at the red rock they were about to collide with. Yesterday, at around the same time, Hank had watched them floating by and from overhearing snatches of their conversation had concluded they were staying down the beach at the Boatslip, probably having taken the ferry over from Boston for a week of sun and partying.

The thing was they were all blonds. Well, blonds of a sort. Their hair ranged from light yellow to a rusty gold. But seeing them next to Erik almost transformed them into brunettes. Erik was truly blond. From the crown of his head to his eyelashes, even to the tips of his toes. A pure daylight blond whose spirit captured the radiance of the fresh air—when it was fresh, like on that evening they'd first met. To Hank, the young men in the inner tube, appearing out of nowhere and directly in his line of vision above Erik's head, seemed like figments of Erik's imagination, or at the very least, afterthoughts.

"Your toenails are getting sharp, Hank. You ought to let me trim them."

"Are you kidding? I can't stand to have somebody clipping away at them. I hate that sound."

"They scratched me during the night. Look ..."

"All right, then." Hank flipped a drop of oil onto Erik's nose. "I can't refuse you anything."

HANK HAD LIVED ALL his life on Cape Cod. He knew no other home than that of the sandy peninsula that stretched out into the Atlantic. He was familiar with every town and hamlet, with practically every marsh and dune. But it never got monotonous, especially not with the ocean lapping at the shore, the water constantly changing, always alluring.

The son of a Hyannis carpenter, Hank had followed his dad into the trade.

After graduating from high school, Hank worked as a handyman, doing jobs all along the Cape and joining his dad in sanding an elementary school in Wellfleet and re-roofing stables near Truro. He finally decided he wanted to specialize in building decks, patios, and outdoor structures for beachfront properties. Once he decided on his niche, he separated from his dad. In more ways than one.

While his dad worked out of Falmouth at one end of the Cape, Hank moved to Provincetown at the other. He could never get the hang of calling it P-town, that sounded too precious. The reason he moved to Provincetown was because he'd decided he wanted to live among the company of other men. Yes, he was gay, if that's what it was called, and he came to accept that fact.

He moved there in his mid-twenties, living in a furnished room on Bradford Street, creating custom furniture pieces for beachfront properties, getting to know the residents, and putting together a trusted list of clients. Eventually he was building decks on those clients' cottages and condos that stretched the length of Commercial Street.

Hank didn't have much of a social life. Played poker and sometimes went sailing with a couple of friends— straight—Sky, a short order cook on the wharf, and Annette, who owned an art gallery in the center of town. Shy, tall and gangly, but reasonably good-looking, Hank scored an occasional pick-up in a gay bar but it didn't go farther than one-night stands. Neither party was interested in more.

Finally, after ten years he bought his own beachfront condo, not far from Captain Jack's Wharf, a prime location in the West End. He happened to get a spectacular deal from a guy who was moving to Amsterdam to be with his new lover. And the irony was, Hank had built the condo's deck himself five years earlier.

IT WAS ONLY A week ago that Erik had been hitchhiking to the Lower Cape. On a clear evening in July. His last ride had taken him within sight of his destination, P-town, and he could see the lights come on in the tower of the Pilgrim Monument, below which were hundreds of other lights from low buildings crowding the beach. To Erik they looked like multicolored stars that had crawled up out of the water to shine on the sand and he longed to be standing among them.

Hank was heading north in his jeep loaded with lumber. He slowed for the boy who was tentatively holding out his thumb.

"Are you going to P-town?" Erik asked uncertainly.

"Provincetown. Of course. It's the last town on the Cape. Nowhere beyond that but the ocean."

"A dumb question."

"Hop in. We'll be there in ten minutes."

"Thanks." He climbed up into the jeep with a sketch pad and his knapsack containing a few clothes and extended his hand to Hank. "My name's Erik and these are all of my earthly possessions."

Hank laughed. "Glad to be of service to you and all that is yours."

Erik smiled. He stuck his head out the window to watch the stars coming out and the hint of a silvered moon. "Beautiful evening."

"That's right. And you've got a lot more beautiful evenings to look forward to. The place is full of them."

"I wouldn't mind that."

Hank watched the wind blow the boy's hair all over the place, straight up into a funnel, then off to the side, now into his eyes. His lithe body was perched on the seat and the wind blew billows up the back of his shirt.

"Where are you from?"

"Springfield." Erik made a disgusted face.

"Is that right?"

"The town itself isn't that bad. But I'm leaving a bad situation. Not to go into it too deep, but I got sick and tired of living with an abusive stepdad and a mom who doesn't see it for what it is. Fights, constant name calling, even him getting physical."

"That's rough."

Erik shrugged and smiled again.

At least he could still smile, Hank thought and more power to him. "Why come to Provincetown?"

"I heard it was an artists' colony ... I do sketches ... and a little painting ... I want to find some other like-minded people to hang out with."

"Yes, it is an artists' colony. You can actually see the light in the air because it's a peninsula surrounded on three sides by water. That's the reason artists come here."

"You can't see light in the air, though."

"You can. I've seen it."

Yes, Hank thought, it was an artists' colony. But it was also a Gay Babylon, that's why most boys Erik's age hitched a ride here, to party. That is, assuming Erik *was* gay. He had an artistic temperament, a sketch pad, and an ethereal quality. That was enough to convince Hank. Yet he'd made no mention of the scene here.

"You know anybody in town?" Hank asked.

"Not yet. But I will. I'll get a job as a waiter. Or clean rooms and make beds or something."

"I don't want to be a prophet of doom but it's hard to find that kind of work at the height of the season. Those gigs are already taken."

"Really?"

"It's seasonal work, you know. Catering to the summer crowd up here, then heading to Key West to do it all over again in the winter. Provincetown and Key West, they're the evergreen resorts on the Atlantic's gay circuit."

No reaction.

"How old are you?"

"Nineteen."

When they reached the center of town, Erik's eyes widened in amazement at the honky-tonk atmosphere surrounding McMillan's Wharf and Commercial Street.

"This is it. The main strip," Hank announced matter-of-factly.

Some loud and rowdy gay guys were piling out of a pot dispensary, a huge placard in the window advertising a Drag-a-Thon this coming Sunday at the Boatslip.

"Is it like you imagined?" Hank asked.

"I expected it would be real quiet."

"Parts are real quiet, like farther down in the West End."

And soon all the bustle was just a brilliant green blur in the rearview mirror. Now the street was lined with dark cottages, and the moon cast its reflection on the water in the harbor.

Hank parked in front of one of the cottages. The sound of breakers was all there was to hear. "Let's get one thing out in the open. You *are* gay, yes?"

"That's right. You?" Erik asked.

"Last time I checked—a few minutes ago," Hank admitted.

"I would have come out to you right away," Erik explained, "only I didn't think you were gay, you don't seem like it, so I didn't know how you'd react."

"Well, I am. You are. And here we are."

"Where are we?" Erik straightened his shirt and brushed the hair out of his eyes.

"At my condo. Remember when I told you there weren't many gigs to be had during the rest of the summer season? You're going to move in with me. At least until you find some work."

Erik looked stunned. "I don't know what to say. Except I'm really grateful. You saved me from sleeping on the beach."

"Imagine that."

So, it's what Hank suspected. Erik was broke. Well, it made sense, a nineteen year old impulsively leaving home.

Hank gave Erik a tour of his condo. The living room and bedroom were side by side. Both had glass panels that led out to a large deck overlooking the harbor. The decor was fairly minimalist. White walls all around. Comfortable sofas in the living room, lamps with wide, coral shades, and silk embroidery on the wall cut from colorful pieces of a kimono. The bedroom featured a ruby-red lacquered dresser, large antique jewel-encrusted swords mounted on the wall, alongside a couple of Japanese woodblock prints. And a large double-sized bed.

"The prints represent two of the Fifty-Three Stations of the old Tokaido Road," Hank explained. "Originally done by someone named Hiroshige."

"So, you know about art," Erik said.

"No. Nothing. One of my clients came over and decorated the place. That's Annette. She owns an art gallery in town, specializes in Asian art and artifacts, and she's a top-notch poker player. We're good pals. So, all I know about art is what she put up on my wall."

"I like the Chinese chest's chrysanthemums and nightingales. Maybe I could sketch them."

Hank set the boy's sketch pad and knapsack down in front of the fireplace. "Maybe you could. You like the place?"

"Sure I do."

"You can do more sketching from the deck out here." Hank bent over to unlock the sliding glass doors.

"Good Lord," Erik said.

"What?"

Erik shook his head. "I didn't realize how tall you were."

"Six-four—but shrinking all the time. Of course, that's what happens when you get older."

"I didn't mean it in a bad way. Being tall is cool."

"No offense taken. Hungry?"

"No."

But Hank could tell he was. "I'll make us something after I unload the lumber from the pickup."

"Can I help?"

"No. I just have to stack it up against the cottage next door. A couple just bought the place and they've hired me to build their deck. Why don't you jump in the shower? The kitchen and bathroom are in the back facing the street. Just down this hall."

"I'd like to go out on the deck first if you don't mind. I'll take a shower later."

"Be my guest. It's a big deck."

Erik blushed—a sexual reference or an innocent description?

Hank disappeared and Erik stepped onto the deck. The long sigh that escaped from him mingled with the sounds of a foghorn and the water lapping at the rocks. His muscles lost their tightness. Out of the corner of his eye, he saw Hank stacking the lumber against the side of the cottage next door.

Erik was in a different world now, miles away from the manhandling he'd suffered at the hands of his stepdad and the dreary terrain of Springfield's Indian Orchard neighborhood. The thousands of stars flung out over the ocean as far as he could see showed him how vast his world had suddenly become. But truth be told, he only needed a small corner of it. A mist of peace crept up on him, subtly, much more subtly than the dark night had crept up on the day.

A WEEK HAD PASSED since that evening ...

Now Erik raised a pair of nail clippers in the air.

Hank groaned. "Oh, no. You found them."

"Come on. It won't hurt."

The blond boys in the inner tube drifted out of sight in the direction of the Boatslip and Hank and Erik were left on the deck with the unrelieved whiteness of late morning.

"I promise you can cut them. Just let me take a dip first. Get this oil off me," Hank insisted.

The bay was tepid and murky in spots, cold and transparent in others. Hank let himself sink to the sandy bottom where crabs fled from him, seeking refuge under red and green algae. He grabbed patches of seaweed, brutally uprooting them, sending them billowing to the surface. Small, rainbowlike fish darted toward him, steering clear just as they reached his chest, escaping along a thin ray of light that cut the dusky water.

Hank pushed himself up from the depths and took a greedy breath of air. Then he languidly stepped out of the water, the sun already heating his wet body, just as Francisco and his wife pulled up to the next-door cottage. From the deck, Erik watched Hank in conversation with the couple.

"Looks like I'll have to go over there and do some work after all," Hank said when he returned to the deck. "At least have a discussion with Francisco and do some initial planning, maybe take some measurements, do some yard work. It doesn't look like rain after all, so I can't get out of it. By the way, they just got back from their honeymoon." He looked longingly at Erik.

"That's all right, go on over," Erik said swiftly, "but first your clipping."

"Why do I feel like Samson?"

"A big hulk like you should be ashamed to be so scared."

"Speaks the surgeon, Dr. Erik."

Erik laid him back on the big double bed, his feet hanging off, and knelt before him on the floor with the clippers. The large bedroom was cheerful, full of light streaming in through the full-length glass doors, beyond which were the deck and harbor. Erik had plenty of light to see what he was doing. From time to time, he'd look up at Hank, lying back, hands behind his head, a curious smile on his face.

Then finally, Erik gave the all clear. "The operation was a success."

"Good. Now come over with me to meet the neighbors."

Hank and Erik walked across the yard to speak with Francisco. He came from a well-known Portuguese family on the Cape and his dad owned a successful restaurant up on Shank Painter Road and a second one in Wellfleet. He'd married Liz who'd been a bartender at the Wellfleet restaurant but had happily left her position to marry into money. Francisco and Liz were busy inspecting the lumber Hank had stacked against their cottage.

"Not starting already?" Liz asked.

"Not by a long shot, no," Hank replied.

He introduced Erik as a friend who was staying with him for awhile. And it was true, Erik thought, they were friends—but nothing more than that, at least not yet, though they slept together in the big double bed. What surprised Erik were the next words that came out of Hank's mouth, that Erik would be his assistant during the construction of the deck.

"Oh," Liz said to Erik with genuine surprise. "You don't look like a construction worker."

"A carpenter," Hank said, laughing.

"That builds muscle and character," Francisco added.

"I'm more of a painter," Erik said, turning red.

"Really?" Liz asked with interest.

"I do sketches and some watercolors."

"That's funny. So do I," Liz claimed. "I have some up on the walls of the restaurant on Shank Painter Road." And as the two of them discussed their common interest, Hank and Francisco walked around to the back of the cottage to discuss theirs.

Hank told Francisco that before he got started he'd like to know Francisco's needs and any specific or desired features he had in mind for the deck before he obtained the necessary permits to begin work. The first step would be to mark the deck layout with stakes and strings, execute a design plan that would meet property line requirements, and then start an excavation and site preparation.

"You know all the ins and outs of this game," Francisco said. "That's why I hired you. Just come over and make whatever inspections you need anytime and then we'll work up a final plan, make sure it complies with local building codes, and go from there."

"Fine by me."

Later that afternoon, Hank fixed Erik some lunch and they relaxed on the deck. Then Hank decided to inspect the backyard of Francisco's cottage and took Erik along.

"I don't know why you said I'd be your assistant," Erik said. "You know I'm not."

"Why not?"

"What would I do?"

"Well, we can start right now doing a little clearing around what's going to be the deck area, pull up some weeds, get rid of vegetation, rocks, and debris, put them in that wheelbarrow over there. Eventually, we'll remove any sod and grass when we dig holes for the footings."

Well, Erik thought, why not? It would be a way he could show his good faith toward earning his keep, and who knew, it might lead to a vocation where he could earn that keep on a more permanent basis. He showed Hank he was game, going to work right alongside him, clearing the ground of unwanted vegetation. Once Liz peered out at them from the sliding glass doors then discreetly disappeared.

"What did you think of them?" Hank asked.

Erik thought they were a good-looking young couple, but it startled him that they were probably only five or so years older than he was, and yet they had this cottage, interests in two restaurants, a car, a nice deck soon to be built overlooking the harbor, and he had nothing.

"I liked them," he answered.

He and Hank kept pulling up weeds and prickly grass. They worked quietly, except for Hank's occasional humming, sometimes to the accompaniment of a bee's buzzing when it intruded on their solitude.

When they saw Francisco and Liz drive off, Hank complained, wiping his brow, "Francisco told me that his wife is really into exotica. She wants a cashew tree, a Baobab, one of those upside-down trees from Australia, and a gingko ... how the hell does she expect to grow all that up here?"

"Maybe she has magic powers we don't know anything about."

"I've never seen her exercise any. She'd better stick with the beach plums everybody else has. They thrive in these environments ... I hope you'll thrive in these environments too."

"I'm not a beach plum."

"But you're a peach."

"Hank ..."

"You've got to get out and see more of Provincetown. I promise you'll like it here. Tomorrow we'll take a drive down to the Land's End where the Pilgrims first disembarked. They've put up a plaque by the jetty wall."

"Not the Pilgrims I presume."

Hank laughed. "Ah, they probably put up some kind of landmark too."

"Yes, a Bible on a stick."

"Clever. But I'd expect nothing less from an expert toe-cutting surgeon."

And they went back to work.

Francisco and Liz didn't return that afternoon. As Erik cleared vegetation in his assigned patch, he noticed Hank looking at him with pride, and a wistfulness. More humming. Cleaning up. No sunset, the brightness just melted into grey, and the sea turned inky. Lights on a distant ship blinking in the distance. Heat lingered, no breeze to disperse it.

Suddenly Hank put his arms around Erik's waist and turned him around to face him. He smoothed the boy's hair and lifted his chin up, and staring intensely at him, whispered, "I love you ... there, I've said it ... I don't know what I'd do if anything ever happened to you ... or if I ever lost you ... I love you so ..."

Then he thought back to that first night Erik had stayed with him ...

AFTER HANK HAD STACKED the lumber against the side of Francisco's cottage, he returned just as Erik came in from the deck. It was his goal to make Erik feel comfortable. He fixed them a quick pasta with tossed vegetables.

"Sparkling water? Wine?" Hank asked.

"Sparkling water, thanks."

"I'll have the same."

Afterwards, Erik went to take a shower and Hank did the dishes. Then he lit some candles in the bedroom. The vanilla scent mingled with the smell of lumber that was still on his hands. He began to undress, keeping an eye on his flickering shadow on the ceiling. He carefully hung his pants and shirt in the closet but kept his briefs on. Cracking open the bedroom door, Hank lay down on the bed and waited in anticipation.

When he heard the shower shut off, he called, "I'm in the bedroom."

Eventually Erik appeared in the doorway, but instead of a towel wrapped around his waist, he was fully dressed again.

"Don't be afraid," Hank said.

"I'm not ..." But he was hedging.

"Come in."

Erik stepped into the room and walked over to a candle and ran his finger above the flame. "I'm pretty tired from that long hitch. I guess I'll go sleep on the couch."

"Are you uncomfortable here?"

"No, I'm not."

"Did you like your dinner? Your shower?"

Erik nodded.

"Did you like being out on the deck watching the stars over the bay?"

"Yes, of course. But when you ask if I'm comfortable, aren't you being a little presumptuous? I've only known you for a few hours, been in this condo even less. This may be a mistake."

Hank was shocked. "Look, I don't want you to do anything you don't want to do. You're free to leave whenever you like. I'll drive you back to the center of town right now."

Erik didn't answer, his eyes still fixed on the candle's flame.

"But," Hank continued, "why don't you at least give staying here a try? In a few days, if you want to leave, I won't stop you and no hard feelings."

Erik looked over at Hank. He was mesmerized by Hank's broad chest glowing in the candlelight, it looked warm, almost disembodied, inviting him to curl up and cling to it ... it seemed for a minute that Hank lying there was a composite of the different men who'd given him a ride up here when he'd held out his thumb ... He thought they'd been helping him escape, but in reality had he been fleeing to them? They'd only been a touch away, like Hank was now. Oh God, he was tired.

"Lie down beside me ..."

"I can't."

"Of course, you can. You mean you don't want to."

"I do, but—"

Hank was on his feet covering the boy with kisses, becoming more and more passionate with each one. Erik responded, the wall he'd built around himself beginning to explode. In his mind's eye, he watched the wall exploding brick by brick, while he held Hank's tongue deep inside his mouth. Now Hank's big hands were unbuttoning his shirt, his pants, until Erik found himself standing there naked and confused. Hank slipped his own briefs off next and edged Erik onto the bed.

"Come on, baby, kiss me," Hank cajoled. "Put your arms around my neck. Hold me tight."

Erik did, but the sensation of being so overpowered frightened him. Still Hank pushed hard with his tongue down Erik's throat, and Erik had no choice but to accept it. Then he felt Hank's fingers playing around his ass, one of his fingers finding the opening.

"Don't." Erik pulled back, freeing himself from Hank. "Oh, please, don't."

But Hank pulled the boy's legs open and shoved his finger inside him.

Panicking, Erik cried out in terror, "No, goddam you, no!"

Hank stopped immediately. He felt numb and icy as he watched with complete surprise the fear in Erik's eyes.

"I told you to stop," Erik shouted hoarsely.

"I did stop." Bewildered, Hank continued, "And I didn't hurt you. I couldn't have."

Erik clenched his teeth and stared at the ceiling. He fought hard to keep tears of humiliation back. He listened to the sound of the candle sputtering. The sound was as angry and staccato as his own words, "Don't you see? Nobody's been up there before. Not even a doctor. I don't like it. I'm scared. It's not natural."

"But you *are* gay. You said."

"If you mean, do I like men? The answer is yes ..."

"I see ... so ..." A wave of regret swept over Hank. "I hadn't realized ..." His lips sought the inside of Erik's thighs, and he showered the boy's tense flesh with kisses. "I'm sorry ... I really am ..."

He knelt on the floor at the side of the bed and gazed up into Erik's eyes, his regret suddenly turning into a wild happiness, the kind that comes after watching your house destroyed piece by piece by a hurricane only to discover a precious diamond in the sand once the wind has blown on. "You're just inexperienced ... I tend to forget that somebody like you can exist ..."

"What do you mean?"

"It's so different here at the town bars with all the games going on ... I'm pegged as a big macho type. Truth is, most of the time I'm standing there with my stomach churning, thankful the bar's there to support me. Christ ... kids as young as you have tried to pick me up plenty of times, but I can see in their eyes that they know everything, have done everything, and want to go on from there ... but there's no place left to go. It doesn't work like that, not for me. I'm not an angel, sometimes I succumb, I'm only human ... but I usually turn away ... there's something about their eyes, about their mouths ... that's dead. That makes me uncomfortable as hell and I find my way home alone."

Erik gave him a small smile. But then he lost it, and his face was deadpan. Still, he didn't stop looking at Hank. In fact, he reached out and rubbed the nape of his neck.

Hank grabbed both of Erik's hands. "I want to go on a voyage of discovery with somebody who hasn't reached the destination yet. So, we can go there together. Does that make sense to you?"

Erik nodded. Tears welled in Hank's eyes. What had he been thinking to have come on so strong to someone who wasn't jaded by sex and drink and drugs, who hadn't spent his young years jumping out of one bed and into another. In fact, somebody who'd fled a situation rife with abuse, who needed a protector, not a seducer.

ANNETTE AND SKY CAME over to Hank's for a poker game, a regular occurrence. In fact, it was the second time this week. And the second time Erik would be joining in. Annette was especially fond of him because he liked to sketch and she loved art. She owned an art gallery in town specializing in Asian art and artifacts and had decorated Hank's apartment. But her expertise didn't involve sketches, so she was in no position to offer Erik any help other than encouragement.

She was posing for him now on the deck, in her red straw hat, trying to keep still, staring out at a buoy bobbing in the distance as Erik did a charcoal of her in silhouette.

Hank and Sky, his buddy who was a cook at a seafood joint on the pier, joined them.

"I thought you were going to sketch corals." Hank indicated the colorful line of them Erik had arranged on the railing.

"I offered to pose," Annette said. "He can do those corals anytime."

"Erik was begging me to sit still the other day so he could finish one of me," Hank said. "I didn't have the patience."

"No way you can sit still, I'll vouch for that," Sky chimed in. "You've always got to be doing, doing, doing."

"That's my DNA," Hank admitted.

"Are salmon steaks OK for tonight?" Sky asked. "I brought some prime ones from the pier."

Everybody agreed and Sky went inside to start cooking.

Hank gazed at the dominant white sky. It was humid again. Unpleasant. He watered the plants on the deck, the morning glories and sand myrtle, then stretched out on his deck chair, popped open a can of beer and took a sip.

Erik, continuing to sketch Annette, said tentatively, "Hank ..."

"I'm listening."

"About dinner and poker. I want you all to eat dinner and start playing without me."

"Play without a card shark like you?" Hank asked.

"I have to go into town and get something." It was Hank's birthday in two days, a semi-big one, thirty-five, and he wanted to go down to the shops around the wharf and get him something.

"OK. But I wish you'd be more specific," Hank said, knowing full well Erik was going hunting for a birthday gift.

"I'm done, Annette." Erik showed her the sketch.

"Good job, Erik. Now I can take this damn hat off and go inside. I'm starting to sweat like crazy."

After Erik left, Hank admitted to Annette and Sky, "I figure he's gone to get me a birthday present."

"You always had a sixth sense, man," Sky said.

"I don't think so. I just know the kind of kid Erik is. He doesn't have two nickels to rub together. He's going to buy me something with the meager salary I gave him for helping to clear out Francisco's back yard."

"Bingo," Sky said. "And he's not spending it on booze or drugs."

"Or even putting it towards a cellphone he probably needs," Hank said.

Annette touched Hank's shoulder. "He's a keeper."

EVENING FELL GENTLY OVER Commercial Street, low, quick-moving grey clouds seeming to pick up the reflections of the colored bulbs strung across the fish palaces and the jabbing spotlights of the outdoor discos.

There was a bit of moisture in the air, and after being so warm, it was cooling down quickly and Erik was glad he'd carried a light windbreaker with him. The sidewalks were full of lovers … families … fishermen coming home. Erik slipped past them all, determined to reach the pier and see what he could find. He passed a small boutique with a blue-and-white linen tablecloth in the window marked SALE. It might look nice on Hank's round table in the living room. But it wasn't exactly what he was looking for.

He turned into a bright artisan's gallery on the pier. Here there was everything. Lamps made from shells, gold watches, neon sculptures, leather belts, a voucher for free tattoos. He circled the gallery twice, then moved on to a marine supply store where all-weather gear choked rack after rack, rubber boots spilled out of cardboard boxes, and utility flashlights hung from the ceiling on twine. A bead of sweat formed on his temple. He'd hoped to get tools or materials that Hank could actually use in his line of work, say a framing square or safety equipment like goggles and gloves. But it was clear he wouldn't find them here.

Suddenly he left the store and, breaking into a sprint, hurried back to the boutique. It was just closing.

The proprietor was about to leave but let Erik in, happy he might get rid of the SALE item, and was quick to sing its praises. "The linen is superb quality. Flown over from Ireland. By way of Boston, of course ... But I don't want to twist your arm."

WITH THE GIFT-WRAPPED PACKAGE securely in his hands, Erik felt exhilarated. He walked west toward Hank's condo, but out of the blue stopped at a spot he'd always admired, a little outdoor café consisting of a tightly-knit group of tables in a garden, set far back enough from the street to provide some tranquility. The problem was it was always full and tonight was no exception, but Erik was lucky enough to catch the eye of a sympathetic waiter who let him sit at a table against the fence where the waiters would pause to verify the payments.

The waiter, an effeminate, sweet reed of a man, was quick off the mark. "Now, you," he addressed Erik, "don't cast those fake doleful eyes up at me. If there ever was a premeditated, unrepentant dessert eater, it's you. I'm Gordon, by the way."

"Erik."

Gordon brought him a chocolate ice topped with whipped cream in a tall, frosted glass.

He noticed the package wrapped in silver and purple paper. "Now, who is getting that?"

"My boyfriend." Erik was surprised, that had just come out of nowhere.

"Oh, really? What's his name?"

"Hank."

"And how are you and Hank getting along?"

Erik just smiled and put his windbreaker on.

Gordon inched onto the chair next to Erik. "I can't sit here too long, too many customers, but I'll look busy, like I'm fixing some mistakes on the bills. With me it's hit *and* miss. This summer is definitely not as good as last. In tips or in men."

Erik nodded, only half listening. He was enjoying it here, letting the sweet ice melt in his mouth and watching the customers laughing and talking, having a good time. Little lanterns hanging from the trees spun colors on the crowd below and a breeze stirred.

"This one guy I'm seeing on and off ..." Gordon continued. "He drinks too much, forgets to text me when he's promised to, lies around the place all day while I'm out hustling for tips, and won't pick up after himself. He buys me flowers to get back in my good graces, then steals my tip money. And I'm sure he plays around while I'm working. Though I don't have any proof."

"He plays around?"

Specks of red light from the lantern above moved up and down Gordon's long fingers.

Erik and Gordon laughed at the dancing rays and Gordon said again, "No, I don't have any proof."

THE LONG WALK HOME was invigorating. Some rain swept in from the sea but stopped after a few minutes. The crowds thinned out and for the last stretch of his walk Erik didn't pass anybody except an old fisherman.

As he rounded the bend to the condo, there was a tapping on the window from the cottage next door. Francisco opened the door and told him to come in. Erik said he should be getting back to the poker game, but Francisco insisted and led him into the kitchen. The floor was covered with hang gliding gear, a couple of parachutes, what even looked like sea diving equipment.

"You have your own store here," Erik said, surprised.

"Only since Liz has gone to her mother's. She won't be back tonight. That's the only reason I can destroy her kitchen." He knelt down, his back to Erik, and attempted to repair a fin that had cracked. "This goddam rubber adhesive sticks to everything. I don't know if this is going to work or not. I'll have to take this fin for a swim and perform some kicks to make sure it can stand the strain of diving."

"Do you need me for anything, Francisco? If not, I have to get back to the others."

"No, I don't need you for anything." Francisco stood up and eyed the present in Erik's hands. He placed it on the counter. "I just wanted to know when you and Hank are going hang gliding with me?"

"You must be joking. You're not going to get me out on one of those things. You could maybe talk Hank into it. Not me."

He grabbed Erik by the shoulders. "Where's your sense of adventure? ... Hey, how about parachuting, then? It's a thrill like no other, jackknifing through the air. Ever tried that?"

"No."

"Or pearl diving. You'd like it. Go down real deep and come up with a handful of pearls." He grabbed Erik's hand and put it on his crotch. Erik pulled away.

"Why'd you do that? Take your hand off me?"

Erik shrugged.

Francisco smiled, showing his perfect white teeth. "Come on, kiss me. You want to. I can tell."

Erik stared into Francisco's handsome face. A lock of his silky black hair fell down across his forehead.

Francisco spoke softly yet forcefully. "I really want to kiss you. I've wanted to ever since I first saw you. Didn't you ever think about me?"

"No, not even once," Erik protested.

"Not once? Not one little moment?" Francisco looked hurt. He licked Erik's ear and whispered in it, "I dreamed about you last night as I slept next to my wife. And I wished it had been you instead of her."

Erik wanted to run away, be anywhere else on earth but here, yet he was frozen. Francisco was so handsome, his olive skin so smooth, his dark eyes piercing, the smell of the sea and sand clinging to him. Erik's body arched with adrenalin and desire and when Francisco's full lips sought his, he gave in, hungrily exploring Francisco's mouth. Before he knew it, his arms were around Francisco's shoulders and he was moaning with passion. The kisses never seemed to stop, he didn't want them to.

"I have to come up for air." Francisco finally broke away. "But we'll be more comfortable in bed anyway."

Shell-shocked, Erik struggled to regain his equilibrium. "I can't ... I just can't."

"Come on, we've got to keep this momentum going. It's terrific."

But now Erik was cold, in his body and his mind, and his desire had disappeared as quickly as it had come. He eyed Hank's present on the kitchen counter. "It's not possible."

Francisco laughed uneasily. "What's wrong? Aren't I good-looking enough for you?"

"You know you are."

"Then what? Because I'm married?"

"Yes," Erik lied. But it wasn't that, it was because of his own guilt. He grabbed Hank's present and left Francisco standing staring at him in disbelief as he walked out the cottage door.

"Here he is," Annette said when Erik came in. "How was your little sojourn?"

"It was nice. I stopped at that outdoor café near the pier and had a chocolate ice."

"Well, you've returned just in time," Hank said, throwing down his cards on the table. "Now you can save me from the clutches of this she-wolf. I'm losing badly to her. So is Sky."

"I'm about ready to fold and call it a night," Sky said.

"No way," Hank admonished him. He noticed the package in Erik's hands and winked at him. "You're not doing a very good job of hiding that." He grinned. "I think I know who that's for."

Erik sheepishly lay the package on a table and went to wash up. When he returned, Hank said, "Here's a chair and a beer for you. Come join us."

"If you don't mind, I think I'll sit this one out. I'm tired. I'd like to go out on the deck for a while then turn in."

Hank reached out and squeezed Erik's hand. "That's OK, baby. You do what you like."

On the deck, Erik stared out to sea, watching the stars fill the sky for miles on end.

THE DAY BROKE BLUE and sunny. Hank opened his eyes to find this welcome change enlivening the room, the sunshine bringing in the reflections of the water to shimmer on the west wall. Hank kicked the top sheet down and let the breeze idle over his naked body. Erik lay asleep beside him, naked too, on his stomach. There was plenty of room for them both to stretch out on the long white sheets.

But now that disturbing image from last night came back. In the stillness, he had thought he'd heard Erik's voice talking to somebody outside and a door shutting. Then a silence. Finally, he'd left the others at the table and stepped outside onto the deck to find out if anything was wrong. That's when he'd seen Erik through the kitchen window locked in Francisco's embrace, kissing him with an unimaginable passion. Dazed, he'd come back inside and joined Annette and Sky at the poker table.

From the bed Hank could see the blue sky dipping down into the bay. Boats with their languid, billowy white sails floated on somewhere.

Suddenly, not permitting himself to hesitate, not even for a moment, for he knew in his heart that a moment's hesitation would change everything, he leaped from the bed and grabbed one of the artifacts from the wall, a twelve-inch curved sword, an antique with a thick blade and rust-encrusted handle with dusty little jewels set in the base. He crawled back into bed, flipped Erik over on his side and nuzzled in behind him, then in one swift movement he turned the blade so it pointed right at Erik's stomach. Erik woke, saw the blade, and his hands grabbed Hank's wrists and with all his strength tried to push the sword away. But Hank was so much bigger and stronger. It was a short struggle. Hank drove the blade through both the boy and then himself so they were skewered on it together, the tip plunging out Hank's back.

Their arms and legs flailed only for an instant and their strangled cries were low and deep, then everything was quiet. The sunlight continued to play over their sprawled, naked figures and the boats still moved on into the blue sea, yet this bed was a brand-new sarcophagus full of ripe blood and beautiful flesh.

Acknowledgments

Many thanks to Harold Schmidt at Tree Line Books who has worked so tirelessly and creatively to publish my work. Thanks also to Roderick Brydon/klrcovers.com for bringing all the design elements together for the cover.

About the Author

JOHN STEWART WYNNE is an American author of fiction, as well as a Grammy-nominated producer of audio books.

In addition to his short story collections *The Other World* and *Consequences of Attraction*, he has written the novels *The Red Shoes* (nominated for the Lambda Literary Award for Best Gay Fiction) and *Crime Wave*. His writing has been praised for its audacious originality, beautiful imagery, the astute asides and wry observations of his characters, and his highly charged but often darkly comic *mise-en-scènes*.

His short fiction has been published in *High Risk 2*, *Christopher Street*, and John Calder's international *New Writing and Writers* series, among other publications.

Wynne's poetry has been featured in *The American Poetry Review*, and his controversial long narrative poem *Two Struggling Actresses*, about an actor consumed by the personality of Jayne Mansfield, appeared in *The Paris Review*.

Tree Line Books first introduced John Stewart Wynne's work to readers when we published the print edition of his story *The Sighting* as the inaugural title in our Tree Line Story Book Series. The series has continued in ebook format with more stories by Wynne: *Louise, Don't Go*; *Narcissist*; *Blonds*; *A Night in the Pampas*; *The Needles Highway; Afternoon;* and *Halloween Card*, as well as the ebook edition of *The Sighting*.

For a complete and up-to-date list of the author's books, visit: *Books2Read.com/John-Stewart-Wynne*

Praise for **THE RED SHOES**
Lambda Literary Award nominee for Best Gay Fiction

"Set in contemporary New York City, this is a beautiful dark queer re-visioning of the Hans Christian Andersen fairy tale. Wynne immediately engages the reader with finely-detailed descriptions, nuanced character development, and an air of mystery that makes this 400+ page text read like a novella.

Wynne takes the reader on the erotic emotional and psychological journey endured, and sometimes enjoyed, by the protagonist. Venturing throughout New York City, he mingles with the rich in Gatsby-like decadence in Manhattan and drug-addicted 'sleazeballs' in dilapidated apartments alike.

The Red Shoes is rife with allusions to Chaucer, Blake, and Milton. Such allusions seem to situate the novel amongst the long tradition of story re-telling and helps to highlight the many intersections between the characters.

In *The Red Shoes*, Wynne elegantly blends spirituality, sensuality, obsession, lust, drug (ab)use, as well as interspersed social and cultural commentary." (LAMBDA LITERARY REVIEW)

"I read this so fast I got blisters turning pages. *The Red Shoes* is so astonishingly good, original, beautiful and amazing ... it's like a sumptuous meal with all flavors—salty, bitter, sweet, hot. I love the Gothic feeling of impending doom and the counterbalancing elements of light. Wynne's writing is free of compromise, fear ... Wynne writes such brilliant back and forth dialogue, and I am astounded at the way he writes about sex—how deep it can go, the different ways it can satisfy. He has the rare ability to write on a plane floating just above life, or below it. And his voice doesn't sound like anyone else's. I think *The Red Shoes* is a great work of art." (Kate Christensen, PEN/Faulkner Best American Work of Fiction Award winner)

"The narrator is as fully realized and endearing a character as I've ever known. The first person worked so well here. The novel is cohesive, charming, sad, and a true achievement. It's really very grand." (Ben Schrank, author of *Love Is a Canoe*)

"I loved the mysteriousness of everything and everybody in *The Red Shoes* and the way its preoccupations with loss, danger and safety would loom in and out of view in the surreal fog of drugs, sex and dark humor. I found it quite haunting and didn't want it to end." (Stephen D. Adams, author of *The Homosexual as Hero*)

"Wynne's compelling re-telling of Hans Christian Andersen's fairy tale *The Red Shoes* is a battle between love and lust, self-abandon and self-redemption. It's an emotional rollercoaster through rat-infested alleys, basement tenements, ostentatious penthouses, lofty museums, and houses of prayer. With remarkable sensitivity, Wynne takes us into the heart and very soul of his character's dilemma, without a sentimental misstep or unmeasured beat." (Janyce Stefan-Cole, author of *Hollywood Boulevard*)

Praise for THE OTHER WORLD

"If there is a bright spot at all to this country's history of puritanical repression, it is in its tradition of 'outsider' art, art fueled by feelings of otherness that have been shared by certain artists [such as] Tennessee Williams, Carson McCullers, and Truman Capote ... And now there's John Stewart Wynne, whose first collection of stories *The Other World* is among the most remarkable books I have ever read.

Wynne's perspective is dark and terrifying and is made all the more so by his stark, vivid descriptions of contorted states of mind and, strangely, by his beautiful, at times lyrical, use of language. His style is disorienting.

There are six stories in *The Other World* and at least three are masterpieces, as good as anything written recently.

This is disturbing stuff, but lovely as well, haunting and powerful. John Stewart Wynne deserves a wider audience, for his is a unique vision. *The Other World* is one of the best books of the decade." (THE JAMES WHITE REVIEW)

"This is a collection that deserves to be savoured. Several stories were even more engrossing when I read them for the second time, and I expect that they will grow even better my third time around.

The Other World stories are full of frights that can be found in any home, neighborhood or culture. We don't need to invent creatures that bump in the night in order to fear the dark. Sometimes human beings are the scariest monsters of all." (LONG AND SHORT REVIEWS)

Praise for THE SIGHTING

"There is nothing else quite like *The Sighting*, for no other writer has experimented with gay experience in the context of our adolescence in straight America in such a direct, sensual and imaginative manner." (GORDON MONTADOR, BODY POLITIC)

"*The Sighting* is absorbingly disconcerting. In its Middle West small town teen-age setting there are sightings of a flying saucer above the town, Bela Lugosi in person appears, and at the climax these two interventions are bizarrely and violently counterpointed against a celebration of sensual love between two boys. The juxtaposition of the surreal and the naturalistic in the denouement is oddly satisfying and miraculously unsentimental in its endorsement of the 'abnormal' relationship." (CHARLES PALLISER, LITERARY REVIEW)

"John Wynne is obviously an exciting talent ... I hope *The Sighting* finds the audience it deserves." (HUBERT SELBY JR., AUTHOR OF *REQUIEM FOR A DREAM*)

"An impressive achievement ... I like *The Sighting* for its strictness, the way it uses facts, its humanity." (YVES NAVARRE, WINNER OF THE PRIX GONCOURT)

Praise for CRIME WAVE

"Wynne's first novel is a disturbing and well written book. Its genre is Manhattan *lumpen* Gothic and it wanders through psychopathic dreams of electrocuted babies and brothels with one-legged tarts, but the book has a compelling and terrible beauty." (BARBARA TRAPIDO, THE SPECTATOR)

"*Crime Wave* is about personal and social sado-masochism. The author's challenging aim seems to be to show that there is no such thing as 'mindless violence,' whether directed towards the self or towards others. *Crime Wave* is an ambitious first novel." (JENNY UGLOW, THE TIMES LITERARY SUPPLEMENT)